An

Robert R. Owens (signature)

America's Trojan War

Dr. Robert Owens

DEDICATION

This book is dedicated to all the heroes who have protected and preserved our freedom, to those who have given the full measure of devotion, to the wounded warriors, and to those Patriots who have not lost hope.

America's Trojan War

America's Trojan War

America's Trojan War

ACKNOWLEDGMENTS

I want to acknowledge Dr. Rosalie Owens. Without her encouragement this book would never have been written and without her expertise and dedication in editing this book would not be what it is.

America's Trojan War

CHAPTER ONE

Setting Suns Dying Embers and the American Dream

The party was winding down. The only people left were Mike's family and a few old friends. After fifty-one years of working Mike Harrigan was finally going to retire. Friday had been his last day at the Ford Stamping plant in Rockville, Maryland. He had worked there for twenty-nine years, ever since he had retired from the Marines. He had given notice this would be his last week as a night watchman at the local National Guard Armory in Rockville, a part time job that had helped pay for his three children to go to college.

Making a toast, Mike's best friend Jim Cummings said, "I want to wish Mike all the best, he has earned some time to himself and if that means I've got to tag along and show him where and how to fish, I guess I can make that sacrifice." Jim and Mike had been best friends since grade school. Jim had preceded

Mike into retirement by three years and he was always bragging that he had finally found the best fishing spots in the tri-county area.

"You may know where to fish but I'll have to show you how," Mike said with a smile as he thought about the fun it would be to spend time doing what he wanted every day.

"I might have a Honey-do list big enough to need Jim's help after all these years of shift work," added Mary, Mike's wife with a smile.

"I might have to get in on that," added Sue, Jim's wife. "I have projects I have been trying to get Jim motivated on since he retired, and all I ever hear about is the big one that got away."

The two couples had been looking forward to Mike's retirement for years. They had all grown up together, raised kids together, and they had so many plans for travel and fun they would have to live to be one hundred to get it all done.

"Is this what I've got to look forward to," said Mike Jr., who everyone called Junior. "I'm going to work for fifty or sixty years and then when I'm done a Honey-do list fit for a maintenance crew."

"You could get a jump on that any time you feel like it," interjected Jean, Junior's wife of twenty years.

"Why does a Honey-do list always turn into a Honey-doesn't list? That's what I want to know," asked Ashley Mike's daughter.

"Hey wait a minute! I've been working on that Honey-do list like a finish painter with a punch list since we've been married. At our wedding Instead of 'I do' I should have said "Honey-do'" laughed Ed, Ashley's husband.

As the conversation swirled around who does what and who needs to do more suddenly they were interrupted as seven of Mike's eight grandchildren burst into the room.

"Mom! Billy won't let me have my turn," little Mike cried as he tried to grab an electronic game out of his brother's hand.

"Billy let your brother have a turn," Jean said without looking up.

"And John hit me," cried Marsha. At seven Junior and Jean's youngest complained about her cousin who was only five.

"John you know you're not supposed to hit girls," said Ed sternly.

"But she hit me first," said John as he ran to his mother.

"That doesn't matter. You don't hit girls and that's that," Ed said in the level tone that told John he was serious.

"I'm sorry," John said as Marsha beamed knowing that she had started it by hitting John but she had won anyway.

And so it went, the back and forth of a happy family surrounded by good friends celebrating a happy occasion. Everyone knew Mike had worked hard. Twenty years in the Marines with two tours in Vietnam when the war was hot then twenty-nine on the line at Ford. He had worked hard and built a good life.

By 11 PM everyone was gone and it was just Mike and Mary as it had been for the last ten years since Ashley and Ed got married. Some called it an empty nest, but Mary called it their second adulthood, the one where they have the health and the means to do what they want in life. She had been trying to get Mike to retire since he turned Sixty-two. She knew with his Marine pension, his Ford pension, her pension from the school district, and both their Social Security they would be bringing in more than when they were raising the kids on two salaries. Mary wanted to travel while they were still young enough and healthy enough to enjoy it.

All along Mike said he was going to wait until he reached sixty-six. So his Social Security wouldn't be penalized just in case he ever had to go back to work. But Mary knew it was really because Mike liked to work, and he couldn't see himself without a job.

He had intended to keep his night watchman job at the armory, but Mary had at last convinced him to let it go so this was his last week. Then he planned a few weeks relaxing and checking out some of Jim's secret fishing holes until after Rockville Days over the Memorial Day weekend where Mike always ran the beer booth for the VFW. On June First they would take off for their first cruise with Mike's two older brothers, their wives, and Mary's younger sister. This was Mary's dream come true, and though Mike would rather stay home and fish he loved doing things to make his wife happy.

CHAPTER TWO

The Sun Also Rises

The last week of Mike's long employment journey flew by. Mike knew he could have filed for his Social Security and Medicare online but he was more comfortable going into the office. He had to wait for them and then come back with more paperwork. It took a few days but at last everything was set, and all that was left were a few shifts at the armory.

Mike had always enjoyed being connected to the armory. After his time in the Marines he had spent a few years in the active reserve and then a few more in the inactive, and in a way he missed it. Being the night watchman at the armory had at least given him a uniform to wear, a reason to carry a gun, and a mission to perform that he could tell himself contributed to the nation's defense. This had been a big part of Mike's life ever since he signed up for the Marines the day after he graduated high school.

He had volunteered for Vietnam as soon as he was out of Basic even though he had been posted to Europe and immediately found himself in the middle of the Battle of Khe Sanh. Then he volunteered for a second tour and spent twelve months on search-and-destroy missions in the mountains and valleys of Central Vietnam including two stints in Cambodia. After that he served as a guard at embassies around the world rising to the rank of Chief Gunnery Sergeant before he retired at thirty-seven.

When he came home he found a job at the big Ford Plant where his father and grandfather had worked. He had many chances to get promoted off the line but he stayed in production and worked in the union as floor steward. He always drove Fords and he was grateful for a great place to work that enabled him to build a good life with his childhood sweetheart and raise three great kids.

Mike was healthy and happy. He was looking forward to enjoying a long retirement surrounded by family and friends. His was the American dream; a life of peace and security, prosperity and hope. He had fought for it. He had worked for it. And he believed it was his by right, and a heritage he could pass on to his children and grandchildren.

The Rockville Armory was the home of the 364th Armored Brigade and the 3rd Squadron of the 6th Air Calvary of the Maryland National Guard. Mike and two other retired Vets guarded the massive five hundred acre compound. The facility was built on the grounds of old Fort Benson which had been there since pre-revolutionary times when it was established as a strong point in the wars with the Shawnee Indians. After that it saw duty in both the War of 1812 and the Civil War. It was said General Lee who had supervised the building of the walls in the 1850s had detoured around the fort, because he knew it was too well built.

The massive walls were gone now, replaced by a twelve foot chain-link fence topped by razor wire. Night after night for more than fifteen years Mike had walked guard duty around the perimeter and between the long rows of silent Apaches, Abrams tanks, Humvees, Bradley fighting vehicles, Strykers, and ten ton trucks. Nothing ever happened, and Mike looked at it as almost free money. All he had to do was stay awake.

The two other watchmen were both longtime friends. Harold Harveson had been one of

Mike's best friends since grade school and Tom Simpson had moved on Mike's block when he was in high school. Both had been working at the armory for years, and the three of them had a set routine. Both of them were also retired military.

There were three positions. One man sat in the guard shack at the front gate which was either warm or cool depending upon the season. One man walked a post inside the building where it was either cold or hot depending on the time of year, but at least he was out of the weather. And the third man walked the perimeter and down the long lines of vehicles and choppers. They rotated positions every two and a half hours with everyone pulling a final three hour shift in the last position. Every day they started in different positions so it always worked out by the end of the week.

It was a good job and considered a plumb position among the locals, not hard work, good pay, and it even provided benefits and a chance to do something for the military.

At lunch they all gathered in the Guard Shack for a half hour. That Friday, Mike's last day, Harold brought in one of his wife's locally famous pineapple upside down cakes. She regularly won best in show at the county fair. It was Mike's favorite cake and it had been ever since Beth Harveson was Beth Thomas and she lived next to Mike growing up.

"Mike, I can speak for both of us when I say we're going to miss you here on the job, but we're both really happy for you" Tom said as he lifted the cup from his thermos in a toast.

"Tom's right. You'll be missed on these long cold nights, and the hot ones too, but we're glad to see one of the good guys grabbing the gold ring for once. You and Mary just enjoy yourselves and don't have a second thought for us poor old working stiffs out here doing the heavy lifting," Harold said with the big easy smile that so often lit up his face.

A few jokes about fishing and of course Honey-do lists and they went back to work. This next to the last shift saw Harold stay in the Guard Shack, Tom head off to patrol the perimeter, and Mike went inside the cavernous building. Even in early May it was still cold in the big building in the wee hours of the night. Mike, just like everyone else, usually made a round and then warmed up in the waiting room of the Commandant's office. And just like everyone else he was reading a book to help him stay awake.

Unlike Harold who read nothing but car magazines or Tom who read History Mike was just settling in to a book by one of his favorite authors Pat Buchanan, *Death of the West*, and he was silently cheering as Pat addressed the many problems of unregulated immigration. Mike was pro-immigration. His own great grandparents had come from Ireland during the potato famine, but he believed people should come in legally and that we should choose the best and the brightest who wanted to become Americans and not people who had no love for America, its tradition, or its people.

CHAPTER THREE

Then the World Came Calling

Tom's two hour shift in the warm Guard Shack was almost over. He had been engrossed in reading a new History of the Revolution that had just come in the mail that day when he was interrupted by a Humvee flying the flags of a Brigadier pulling up to the gate. He couldn't remember the last time anyone had driven up to the gate during his shift. He thought it was back in July of last year when the Kilderson boy pulled up thinking he was at the UPS depot which was on the other side of town.

Tom got up and walked out of the Guard Shack and called through the gate, "Hey who's there?"

The sergeant driving leaned out of the window and replied, "This is General Edward Davidson, the Inspector General of the Maryland National Guard here for a surprise inspection."

Tom had heard of General Davidson, and he knew he could make an inspection any time he wanted so he went back in the Guard Shack and pressed the big red button that opened the electronic gate. He walked outside again to greet the General and see if there was anything he needed Tom to do. As the Humvee pulled up next to Tom he said, "Good morning General and welcome to the Rockville Armory. Is there anythi" which is as far as Tom got when the driver reached out of the window holding a Glock 17 with a suppressor and shot Tom between the eyes.

Immediately, two men dressed in the same guard uniform Tom was wearing exited one from each side of the vehicle. One dragged Tom's body into the Guard Shack as the other keyed a radio mic on his shoulder and said, "The door is open" in Arabic. In a few moments what seemed like an endless line of headlights appeared around the bend and began moving towards the gate.

The man dressed as General Davidson stepped out of the Humvee. It pulled out of the way as the first vehicle of the convoy rolled into the armory. The vehicles were a motley collection of vans, SUVs, trucks big and small, cars, school busses, a few Greyhounds, and other commercial busses. One after another they pulled in and headed through the streets of the armory to the big central building.

As Harold rounded the corner and came to the front side of the compound he could see and hear the vehicles coming into the armory. "Now what's all this about," he said, as he picked up his pace and headed along the fence towards the Guard Shack. "Why didn't Tom radio me there was traffic," he wondered as he passed the silent shadows of Apache helicopters huddling like giant hornets quilted in darkness.

Harold was about half way from the corner where he had first seen the traffic to the Guard House when suddenly two men came out from between the last Apache and a ten ton truck. They were dressed as MPs. "What's going on guys, is this a dri" which is as far as he got when the taller of the two men raised his hand and shot Harold in the face with a forty-five. The report of the pistol sounded like an explosion in the still morning. It reverberated off the parked ordinance in the clean crisp air like a thunder clap.

"That sounded like a gun," said Mike as he dropped his book and stood up. Keying his radio he said, "Tom is there any trouble at the gate?" When Tom didn't come back right away Mike keyed the radio again, "Harold can you raise Tom?"

Just then he heard the big overhead door of the building open. From his vantage point in the waiting room of the commandant's office at the top of a long flight of metal stairs he could see vehicles pulling in and hundreds of men running into the building. He pulled his gun and crouched down as he heard what he thought was Arabic being yelled between the men as they fanned out through the building.

"This is bad, this is real bad," Mike thought as he quietly made his way back into the waiting room. He knew his radio wouldn't raise anyone at this hour. It was a proprietary frequency. It had a very limited range. He knew he had to warn someone. He had to get the word out that someone was breaking into the armory. As he crawled into the furthest corner from the door he could hear men running up the metal stairs.

In the darkness of the corner he pulled out his cell phone but he only dialed 9-1 when two men in fatigues burst through the door yelling something in what sounded like Arabic. Mike dropped his phone, grabbed his Glock 20 in both hands and began firing towards the door as he rolled to the left behind the big metal desk of the Commandant's receptionist.

One man was hit and fell face forward into the carpet. The other man raised an AK-47 and began spraying the room. Mike leaned to the right side of the desk and fired again. The second man dropped but two more were crowding into the room. One man got off a short burst before Mike unloaded his remaining fifteen rounds into both of them. Ducking behind the desk Mike pushed the release dropping his spent magazine as with the other hand he pulled out another from his belt. Slamming it into place he was just ready to fire as the next two men ran into the room.

Their AKs lit up the room. Mike hit one man. The man dropped and Mike kept firing. The other man made a run across the room at the desk where it was obvious Mike was taking refuge. More men were coming into the room. As the running man leapt over the desk firing down Mike rolled onto his back and sent two rounds crashing through his body which fell on Mike along with the AK. A round had pierced Mike's left shoulder and the weight of the man pressed him to the ground. He was trying to push the man off him when someone dressed in fatigues stepped around the desk and crashed in Mike's face with the butt of his AK. At the same time another man stepped around the other side of the desk and firing right through his dead companion shot Mike more than ten times. His last movements were involuntary twitches as the bullets entered his body. His last thoughts were of his wife and that he had failed in his duty to protect the armory.

In Arabic a man by the door said into a microphone suspended at his shoulder, "The last infidel is dead."

CHAPTER FOUR

Wake the Sleepers Prepare to Strike

Following an intricately devised plan as soon as the armory was secure a text message was sent out to local sleeper cells.

At four in the morning Achmed Dagher who moved into Rockville four years ago and bought a local convenience store woke the two men who had been pretending to be his brothers. They gathered the many guns and ammunition they had purchased with the profits from the store and loaded them into their Land Rover.

Across town Akeem Kassab who had arrived three years ago and was employed as a driver for Rockville Oil, loaded his Springfield 1911. He put two extra magazines in his coat pocket, left his home in Shinning Hills, a suburb of Rockville, and drove to the oil terminal.

At WNNA the local radio station Ali Shamoun stepped over the body of Dale Thomas the night time DJ as he went to lock the front door.

At the same time Amal Qureshi, the newest recruit to the Montgomery County Police and a graduate of Rockville High and Montgomery Community College who was also a recent convert to Islam, stepped into the station's radio room.

Jim Jordan, the officer currently manning the station's communication hub, turned around to see who was coming in as Amal entered.

"How's it going Jim," Amal asked Jim as he entered the room.

"Trying to stay awake," Jim answered as he turned back to the magazine he was reading.

"Me too," Amal said as he stepped up behind Jim.

"I know wh," was all Jim could get out before Amal slit his throat. After killing Jim Amal sent a text to four men waiting outside the front door: "Now."

The men entered the Montgomery County Police station and walked up to the bulletproof glass of the reception area. "What can I do for you gentleman," Eddy Olson a twenty-three year veteran of the force asked. Waiting for an answer he paid no attention when Amal stepped into the cubicle and plunged his dagger into the side of his neck. Amal then pushed the button that opened the door.

By the time the four men had entered through the steel reinforced door they all had pistols in their hands. "The other two are in the breakroom down this hall third door on the left. You take them out and I will man the radio," Amal said.

After Amal entered the radio room he ordered one of the two radio cars to come back to the station and the other one to report to the guard house at the armory and speak to the guard there about a possible break-in. He had just finished his calls when one of the four men entered the radio room now wearing a Montgomery County Police uniform, "Amal, we've taken the other two out. I will wait outside for the arrival of the patrol car" he said in Arabic.

The squad car arrived at the Station and as the officer walked towards the front door one of the four men stepped out of the shadows and shot him in the back of the head dragging his body back into the shadows. He then climbed into the squad car and drove towards the Oil Depot.

Tim Garrett was a ten year veteran on the

force. As he pulled up to the armory he saw lots of activity. Lights were on and he could hear the big diesel motors warming up even with his windows up. He was a Lieutenant in the 251st Mechanized Infantry and he hadn't heard anything about any maneuvers or night work, so he was on his guard when he pulled up to the Guard Shack. Rolling down his window he asked, "Who're you? Where's Tom, Mike, or Haro," was all he got out before the guard raised his hand holding a 357 Magnum and shot Tim in the head. As Tim slumped on the wheel his foot came off the brake and the car lurched forward and crashed into a truck sitting twenty feet inside the gate.

And so began the first invasion of America since General Ross burned the White House in 1814. Abu Omar al-Baghdadi, the first Emir of the Islamic State, laid the ground work for what was about to unfold. He used the meticulous planning and the ability to establish and maintain networks of operatives connected through social media honed during his time with Al-Qaeda fighting the American occupation in Iraq.

Through the death of the first Emir and the selection of his successor Abu Omar al-Baghdadi the actual establishment of a quasi-state, embracing parts of Iraq and Syria continued. The planning of the assault upon America and placement of operatives also continued. The great refugee crisis opened the door for masses of suicide troops to converge on America not only welcomed by the government but transported and supported. America's leaders believing global warming more of a threat than radical Islam and believing in mass immigration for many reasons welcomed hundreds of thousands. Barely 10% were trained and committed Islamic State Warriors. That was enough to bring the war home to America.

Now a little over twenty thousand well trained Islamic State suicide warriors who had insinuated themselves amongst the Syrian Refugees were leaving the many places the American government had provided for them to live across the country. They converged on four armories that surrounded Washington, DC. These imported storm troopers were augmented by thousands of sleeper cells and radicalized citizens. With meticulous planning and abundant funding, these dedicated men and women executed a plan designed to bring America to its knees.

CHAPTER FIVE

Fire and Sword

"I want the Apaches in the air now!" shouted Bassam Kassab, the man who was dressed as an American General and who was the leader of Strike Force One, to his radio man. Moments later all eighteen Apaches leapt into the air. Following their pre-arranged orders six of the copters stayed over the armory, two flew off to the Oil Depot, two to the police station, and the rest began patrolling the perimeter of Rockville.

Two busloads of warriors arrived at the Oil Depot. They were busy filling every available tanker. More warriors, all in Montgomery County police uniforms, arrived at the station house. At the armory, tanks and Bradley fighting vehicles were being loaded onto transport trucks. Supply crews were distributing arms and ammunition to the thousands of warriors who were still arriving in buses, cars, and trucks.

As the main body of warriors worked to get the Brigade and the oil supply column ready to move small strike teams escorted by Montgomery County Police cars fanned out into the sleeping neighborhoods around the armory. Breaking into houses and using pistols with suppressors they shot the men and older boys then roughly herded the women and children out to waiting busses. Moving quickly from house to house they soon had six buses filled with hostages which they drove back to the armory to join the large convoy which was forming up. Several survivors were able to call the police for help. In moments warriors dressed as Montgomery County police silenced these few.

Within two hours of Tom being shot at the gate the highly coordinated assault by more than five thousand trained and dedicated ISIS warriors, all sworn to fight to the death, turned itself into a convoy of a full mechanized brigade with an air cover that was leaving Rockville and driving with a police escort down US 270 towards Washington, DC.

This scene was replicated three more times in Vienna, Virginia on I-66; Bristol, Maryland on Highway 4; and Calverton, Maryland on I-95. By dawn the four ISIS Strike Forces were speeding towards Washington DC and what they saw as a holy mission to take fire and sword to the capital of the West and the seat of all they despised.

With seven years on the Maryland State Patrol Ron Rousseau thought he had seen just about everything that could possibly roll down I 270. That is until a seemingly endless convoy of military vehicles escorted by Montgomery County PD patrol cars started rolling past his favorite speeder blind.

He immediately radioed, "Montgomery County PD this is State Patrol 734, what's going on?"

"State 734 this is Montgomery County PD. We have been nationalized by the DHS as part of the first ever full scale DC drill. This is extremely high security. It is on a need to know basis only. Do not...Repeat...Do not notify anyone about this drill. Secrecy is imperative." The convoy continued to roll on as Apache helicopters roared overhead.

Following protocol Ron immediately contacted the district post. "Headquarters, this is 734. I am at mile marker 114 and there's a large convoy of military vehicles moving south fast. Do you know anything about a DHS drill?"

"Base to 734 we have no knowledge of a DHS

drill here."

"734 to Headquarters the convoy is being escorted by a Montgomery County PD patrol car. Montgomery County PD contacted me and said it's a top secret drill on a need to know basis. They even told me not to notify you."

Just then a hellfire missile from one of the Apaches slammed into State Patrol car 734.

"Base to 734 how many vehicles are you talking about? Base to 734. Come in 734." When there was no response, the post commander ordered every asset ahead and behind of the convoy to intercept. He also contacted the Montgomery County PD and asked for clarification.

"This is Montgomery County PD to State Police Post 710. The convoy you're asking about is part of a top secret DHS drill. Your reactions and your cooperation will be judged in the final analysis. Your trooper 734 has been physically contacted by DHS operatives and ordered to join the escort. Complete and total radio silence is imperative. There should be no interference with this drill. Repeat. No interference."

It would be more than an hour before another State Patrol officer located the smoking ruin of

Car 734. By then events were moving far beyond the assassination of one officer and the destruction of one patrol car.

CHAPTER SIX

What Can't Happen Here Has

On December 7, 1941 the Japanese could not believe that they were actually able to catch the United States napping at Pearl Harbor. Of course they had done everything they could to achieve this surprise, however there had been so much going on in the last year: the war in China, America's ultimatum, and of course the long and obviously drawn out negotiations in Washington between the two governments. They had planned to have a declaration of war in the hands of the United States government before the attack. So they did not expect to find the Hawaiian Islands without any protection whatsoever.

In August of 1996, Osama bin Laden had issued his first fatwa against the United States and Israel. It was a thirty page polemic entitled "Declaration of War Against the Americans Occupying the Land of the Two Holy Places" that was published in a London newspaper.

There was a second fatwa published on February 23, 1998i. This fatwa was not issued by Osama bin Laden alone. This fatwa was signed by Osama bin Laden; Ayman al-Zawahiri, leader of the Jihad group in Egypt and al Qaeda second-in-command; Abu-Yasir Rafa'l Ahmad Taha, leader of the Islamic Group; Sheikh Mir Hamzah, secretary of the Jumiat-ut-Ulema-e-Pakistan; and Fazlul Rahman, leader of the Jihadi Movement in Bangladesh.

Both of these declarations of war were published before the bombings of the American embassies in Africa and the attack on the USS Cole. Despite two declarations of war and two subsequent attacks everyone in the United States, including our government, was taken completely by surprise when our sworn enemies turned our own planes into WMDs.

By 2016 America had been dedicated to contain, degrade, and destroy the Islamic State. For more than four years many people had warned that the administration's plan to bring in hundreds of thousands of refugees from Syria was like bringing the Greek's gift horse into Troy. Many had pointed to the attacks in France and the compelling evidence such as the Islamic State's own promise to send their warriors in amongst the refugees that this was a mistake of colossal proportions.

However an administration that had won re-election with the slogan, "GM is alive and Osama is dead," who had campaigned on their prowess of defeating terrorism to the point that no one was left on the court but the JV team, marginalized and ridiculed anyone who was brave enough to issue unheeded warnings. Led by a president who would not even say the words, "Radical Islamic Terrorists" and a president who looked out at a world engulfed in terrorist aggression in Africa, Europe, and Asia and said over and over that man-made global warming was our greatest security threat. He even said that he thought man-made global warming was the cause of terrorism and that the bravest thing we could do to confront the terrorists was to conclude a carbon reduction treaty. The pro-state corporations, once known as the Mainstream Media, trumpeted the president's lines and ridiculed any who disagreed.

They contorted facts; however, they had to in order to say there was no organized terrorist threat in America. Just as every president was always killed by a lone crazy person anyone who committed a terrorist act was a lone wolf and most obvious terrorist acts were called instead such things as "A man caused disaster," "Random violence," or "Workplace violence."   Whatever it was they knew it wasn't an organized terrorist threat in America because the President said it wasn't. Implicitly saying over and over, "It can't happen here."

As America slumbered evil plotted and planned. Enemies infiltrated and stockpiled. Warning after warning was ignored and discounted. Like a person with ADD America would wake up after every attack and then lose focus as the next shiny object was dangled in front of their eyes. Global warming, infrastructure, healthcare, and whatever it was we majored on minors concentrating on peripherals as deadly forces aimed at our heart and waited to bring death and destruction designed to turn the American dream into a nightmare.

CHAPTER SEVEN

Beheading a Sleeping Giant

The four columns barreled down America's magnificent highways. By a combination of bluster, bluff, and force they avoided any interference from police or any other of the many forces that were meant to protect the Homeland.

At exactly forty minutes after the four columns hit the highways the four captured radio stations began emergency broadcasts. WNNA in Rockville began announcing that a terrorist attack was underway in Fredrick, Maryland. WOSK in Vienna Virginia began announcing that a terrorist attack was underway in Manassas, Virginia. WWNI in Bristol, Maryland began announcing that a terrorist attack was underway in Annapolis, Maryland. WGNR in Calverton, Maryland began announcing that a terrorist attack was underway in Baltimore. All four stations also sent the information on to their respective networks, the UPI, and Reuters all of which began spreading the stories along to all their outlets: radio, television, and print.

At the same time the four captured police departments reported massive movements of armed men heading towards the locations reported by the radio stations. Simultaneously company sized groups of warriors who had been arriving at the police stations since their capture began fanning out around the stations occupying an area large enough to provide a perimeter several blocks in diameter.

They systematically went from house to house killing everyone. Once they had an area they felt was defensible they began rigging all the buildings with explosives and booby-traps using cars and trucks to barricade streets as snipers took their places on roof tops and waited for their opportunity to die a martyr's death. The warriors who captured the police stations acting as the shock troops for the defense of their now sizable fortified area hit the streets with the armored vehicles and other tactical equipment that had been so generously supplied by America's Defense Department.

As the perimeter was established around the police stations other company sized groups of ISIS Warriors arrived at the local airports in all four locations. All of them were civilian airports, and all four were homes for large corporate fleets complete with numerous jets and fuel supplies far greater than found at most local airports. With ease the ISIS terrorists swept aside the nominal security found at all four airports, and within moments established complete control of the facilities establishing a defense perimeter with the invaders rapidly digging in behind hurriedly established barricades made of vehicles.

As soon as the control towers were in ISIS hands they began filing flight plans for the corporate fleets each airport housed. Each plane was being sent as a manned missile to a different city. Hurriedly the planes were fueled up with enough for one way trips to their locations. They were quickly airborne and on their way.

Everything was going according to plan, and everything was coming off without a significant hitch. Abdal El Shallub, the over-all commander and the one appointed by the Great Emir Abu Omar al-Baghdadi himself as the Governor of the Islamic State Province of America knew this could not continue. Every moment he expected to hear his columns had been engaged by the unbelievers. Every moment that passed without that happening was a moment closer to victory.

Abdal had been in Washington for more than two years. He was employed as an Arabic translator and consultant by the Department of Homeland Security. During his time in Washington besides filtering everything he translated and all the consultation he had offered through his inner ISIS bias he diagramed, measured, and reconnoitered the entire DC Area. He even established GPS coordinates for all his intended targets.

As the sun was rising in a brilliant blaze of red and purple the four columns made it to the beltway. As they began crashing through traffic and running over cars that couldn't get out of the way the alarms began going off. Police and other emergency first responders were being dispatched to the four areas. This was happening just as the captured radio stations began broadcasting their emergency messages.

In short order the columns crossed the beltway easily brushing aside any police who happened to arrive. Following the master plan, all four brigades quickly occupied four major hospitals in the DC area. Strike Force One from Rockville crashed through the gates of Walter

Reed. Strike Force Two from Calverton zeroed in on the Adventist Healthcare Campus. Strike Force Three from Bristol was moving into the large St. Elizabeth complex. Strike Force Four from Vienna easily subdued any resistance and gained control of the great Virginia Hospital Center.

All of these locations were chosen for several reasons. All of them occupied enough space to receive an entire armored brigade. All of them had significant defensive assets such as concrete barriers and strong fences both of which could help in the defense of the facilities when manned by well trained and well-armed combatants. Like clockwork, the men all flew to their assigned tasks. Those acting as the MP sections of the brigades began establishing a presence on the perimeters. The Tanks and Bradley Fighting Vehicles were unloaded, the self-propelled guns were positioned, and machine gun squads fanned out around the perimeter as the engineers began moving the concrete barriers to their most important positions.

Companies of infantry went through the hospitals rounding up everyone: doctors, nurses, orderlies, everyone, and herding them into large rooms were they could be guarded by just a few men. Any security guards were killed. In all of this as was expected many people were able to call 911 and other sources to let people know what was going on. Police were already assaulting the perimeters with little affect.

With the many spurious radio and now network reports of attacks at many different locations the authorities were stunned and confused. In short order the tanks and self-propelled guns roared to life. Timed to perfection just as the guns began to bark the corporate jets began crashing into major hospitals in Richmond, Virginia; Baltimore, Maryland; and Harrisburg, Pennsylvania. Simultaneously, using mortars the forces holding the perimeters of the captured police stations began firing in all directions and began shelling the towns aiming first and foremost at the hospitals.

All of this caused a massive tie up in communications as people tried to sort out what was happening. It was nothing to what was about to happen. The invaders had come equipped with the exact GPS coordinates for all their primary and secondary targets. These had been programmed into the Abrams and the self-propelled Howitzers, making their fire dead-on accurate.

The Abrams Tanks and self-propelled howitzers
of Strike Force One and Two concentrated their
combined firepower on the White House.
Strike Force Three zeroed in on the Pentagon.
Strike Force Four first took out all the bridges
across the Potomac. They then joined Strike
Force Three in bombarding the Pentagon. The
Apache Longbows of all four Strike Forces
launched their full complement of Hellfire
missiles at the chosen targets of their
respective units.

All four positions were now under a growing
attack by local police forces including Swat
Teams. The police were no match for the
heavy machine guns, the Bradley Fighting
Vehicles belching out 25 MM rounds at two
hundred per minute, and the concentrated fire
of whole companies of infantry. The burning
buildings surrounding each facility soon began
to create a no man's land of death. The dead
and dying first responders valiantly tried to
face down America's own weapons in the
hands of those our government had told us we
must rescue.

Abdal El Shallub sat back in the director's office
at Walter Reed. He had joined Strike Force
One as soon as they were in the city, and now
he was surrounded by his lieutenants. Tables

had been brought into the big office and maps of the city were spread everywhere. Preplaced spotters from around the city were calling in the first results of the bombardment.

"The White House is flat, nothing but a smoking crater," shouted one communications expert with joy.

"Order Strike Force One and Two to move their fire to Congress," Abdal ordered.

"The bridges are down and the Pentagon is burning and consumed in flames" another communications man reported.

"Order Strike Forces Three and Four to target Fort Lesley McNair, Bolling Airforce Base, and every other military facility in the area. When they have placed a salvo on each tell them to move on to every police station in DC and Arlington," Abdal ordered as another aid handed him a phone saying, "It is General Malouf."

"General I want your martyrs ready to deploy as soon as their targets open," said Abdal.

"Yes Excellency," replied General Malouf.

"Order all Apaches except for one left for air cover at each position to attack Andrews

Airforce Base," Abdal said as he poured over maps. The sound of gunfire was continuous and the roar of the Apaches overhead almost deafening, but in the silence of his mind Abdul laughed, "We have done it! We have beheaded the sleeping giant."

"Sir our spotters report that Congress has been wiped off the map."

"Excellent! Order them to move on to the Supreme Court. After two salvos tell them to cease fire and conserve ammunition for defense."

"When the Unbelievers wake up today they will be in a new world. No longer will they sit secure behind their oceans while our people die. Today they die and the Caliphate will take its place as Allah's victorious weapon trampling the Crusaders and their polluted culture into their own blood stained dirt!" Abdul shouted in triumph.

Cheering "Allah Akbar! Allah Akbar!" the assembled staff of the first ISIS Province of America gloried in their victory as Americans woke up in a whole new world.

CHAPTER EIGHT

America Under Siege

As the sun rose Washington, DC was a column of smoke on the horizon. Burning craters marked where the day before had stood the White House, Congress, the Supreme Court, the Vice Presidential residence at the United States Naval Observatory, the Pentagon, Fort McNair, Andrews, and Bolling Air Force Bases. All the Washington area bridges across the Potomac were down. Four major Hospitals were turned into enemy bases filled with an armored brigade equipped with America's highest tech weapons with thousands of hostages and enough ammunition and fuel to stand against all comers.

In addition at the points of origin of all four brigades stood captured police stations with defensive positions blocks wide as well as four captured and fortified airports. Just as the sun stretched its first pink fingers over the horizon the large oil depots found in each location were blown up taking out entire neighborhoods and igniting massive blazes that threatened to turn into firestorms.

At the same time as the first shells landed on the White House pre-positioned assassination squads burst into the homes of Cabinet Secretaries, killing everyone they could find within.

The purple tinged red dawn was streaked with the pillars of smoke marking something far beyond a terrorist attack. From the International Space Station one astronaut commented later that it looked like a giant thumb had rubbed an oil smudge where Washington used to be.

As bad as all this was it was only the beginning. All of the details would never be known until long after the dust had settled and the bodies were counted.

America had underestimated the Islamic State ever since President Obonyo had christened them the JV team. At every opportunity the administration didn't seem to take them or the threat they posed seriously. Our lead-from-behind strategy, which some people derisively called "Following," built a Coalition of the "Willing" made up of States who were willing to do nothing beyond join the coalition and ask for increased military aid and money to do so. Then they launched a massive air campaign that dropped most of its bombs in the empty desert because of the hands-tied-behind-their-back rules of engagement. And in a jaw-dropping display of either incompetence or collusion they spent hundreds of millions of taxpayer dollars to train less than a dozen so-called moderate Islamists. These Moderate Islamists immediately turned all their weapons over to the Islamic State and pledged allegiance to the Caliph as soon as their training was complete. One ignored pundit remarked, "The difference between a Radical Islamist and a Moderate Islamist is that while a Radical Islamist wants to cut your head off a Moderate Islamist wants the Radical Islamist to do it."

The same intelligence services which had warned of the WMDs in Iraq told us with great authority that the Caliph commanded less than twenty or thirty thousand volunteers, a ragtag force of amateurs. He actually had a fanatical army of more than 150,000 who were training every day using the latest American technology including Abrams tanks, Bradley Fighting Vehicles, Apache helicopters, and Self-Propelled Howitzers. And this did not include armies reigning and training in Libya, Nigeria, the Sinai, and Yemen.

Strategic leaks from these same intelligence agencies to the mainstream media constantly told us our enemy was mired in the Twelfth Century. Yet we could not keep up with their use of social media, their encrypted communications, or their ability to out think us at every turn. A tone-deaf administration was attempting to conduct a symphony of responses and the orchestra didn't know what to play.

From day one the Islamic State planners, many of whom had been raised in the West, plotted and planned to exploit America's open borders and suicidal immigration and refugee policies to bring the war home to the United States. Almost immediately they began infiltrating warriors through the Mexican border and actively working in masques across America to radicalize people, especially the young and converts. Some of their warriors purposely committed crimes, surrendered and pled guilty so they could recruit in the prisons. They made alliances with the drug cartels south of the border providing them with money and training eventually building a large training camp within fifty miles of the border.

Building impenetrable networks of operatives and sleeper cells all over the lower forty-eight States all waiting for the mass influx of refugee infiltrators their sympathizers and agents within the administration worked tirelessly to materialize. Yes, most of America was lulled to sleep by a complicit media and an administration determined to impose upon the old America they hated its anti-colonialist comeuppance on its way to a new fundamentally transformed America.

Stage One was as much a success as Pearl Harbor and 9-11. Its mind numbing smoke, stench, and screams were just beginning to wake America up when Stage Two exploded with a vengeance.

Terrorists all over the world began attacking American bases, embassies, and businesses. With truck bombs, suicide vests, and snipers the entire American foreign apparatus was under attack. Everywhere radio stations were seized. Soon broadcasts in dozens of languages began declaring the beginning of the world-wide offensive against the American Empire. The followers of the Caliph urged any and all who hated the Yankees to rise up and "Throw off the oppressors."

Hamas declared itself the Palestinian Province

of the Islamic State and launched attacks on Israel from Gaza and the West Bank.

Thousands of infiltrators among the refugees in Jordan overwhelmed their guards and began marching on Amman joined by tens of thousands of armed Palestinians from the generations-old refugee camps where they had been penned up since 1948. The Muslim Brotherhood rose up in Egypt joined by the Sinai Province of the Islamic State and seized military bases as thousands of Libyan ISIS Warriors poured across the border heading to Cairo. In Nigeria, Boko Haram lashed out in its typical brutality in dozens of towns and villages. In Yemen, Al Qaeda in the Arabian Peninsula announced they were the Islamic State Province of Arabia and sent thousands of warriors on the road to Mecca.

Paris, Rome, Amsterdam, and London were ablaze. Sweden was racked by rioting and attacks on the police and the monarchy itself. Refugees, in Germany spreading out like swarm of locusts from their loosely guarded camps, spread death and destruction far and wide. Massive surges of people rounded up and forced from their homes in Northern Mexico were herded across the open border as human shields for large and well trained Cartel formations.

The whole world held its breath as World War III landed with both boots on the heads of America and its allies with a shout of "Allah Akbar!"

CHAPTER NINE

The Giant Awakens

To say pandemonium reigned at the North Atlantic Military Division Headquarters, North American Aerospace Defense Command, and every other command in the American military would be to underestimate the confusion. For a nation with a huge military establishment, a General Staff, and its own intelligence agency, for a nation with tens of thousands of FBI agents all over the country, for a nation with an international spy agency that battled the vaunted KGB for decades it was amazing how badly ISIS caught us unawares.

Reports poured in. Washington was under siege. The White House was a smoking ruin as were numerous other emblematic structures that symbolized America. In Baltimore, Richmond, and Harrisburg massive fires were engulfing large regional hospitals.

General David Callaway Commander of the North Atlantic Military Division was wide awake by the time he arrived four hours earlier than normal at his office at Fort Hamilton in Brooklyn. He had been receiving updates ever since he was contacted at 6 AM by the overnight duty officer.

"Simmons have you been able to raise General Davis at the Pentagon?"

"No sir. I can't contact General Davis or anyone at the Pentagon."

"What about the White House?"

"No sir."

General Callaway was a thirty year veteran who had seen service in both Gulf Wars leading front line troops into battle. He had also served as one of the chief architects of the surge which could have pacified Afghanistan if its announcement hadn't been followed in the same speech by the news that America was going to exit by a date certain. He knew about war first hand and he had surrounded himself with battle hardened commanders.

"Simmons get me Colonel Stamper," Callaway ordered.

"Sir, Colonel Stamper has just cleared the gate and he is on his way up," responded Simmons.

"Good! Send out the order for everyone to report to duty. Schedule a staff meeting for 9 AM. Alert the Governor of every State in the Division that we're nationalizing the Guard to full mobilization immediately. Contact the Airforce and tell them I want AWACS in the air over Washington now, and get me the latest satellite photos immediately. "

"Yes Sir!" Captain Simmons answered sharply as he turned and went to his office to carry out the General's orders.

General Callaway went to the communications room to personally direct and monitor all attempts to raise the civilian government and the Joint Chiefs.

"Have you been able to raise anyone in Washington Sergeant?" asked the General as his concern grew.

"I've been able to contact several Departments but not the White House or the Pentagon."

"Have any of the departments you contacted had a Secretary on site?"

"No sir," answered the sergeant while still monitoring the incoming communication.

Callaway knew that if the President had been

taken out civilian leadership would have to follow the line of succession. He also knew the President had called all his major leaders and supporters to Washington to celebrate what he was calling his "Victory over ISIL." There had been such a long lull in terrorist activities and such a profound cessation of military operations on the part of the Caliphate over the last several months that President Obonyo had declared they were not only contained, they were degraded and about to begin retreating. In his prime-time address to the nation less than a week ago he had gone so far as to paraphrase Winston Churchill when he ended his speech saying, "This may not be the beginning of the end, but it is at last the end of the beginning."

Everyone was there for the celebrations: the Vice President, all the Cabinet Secretaries, and the Joint Chiefs. Everyone had been called to bask in the reflection of the man they were saying was the greatest Commander-in-Chief since Lincoln, Wilson, or FDR as he took an extended victory lap through speeches and parades. Callaway also knew with all these leaders in Washington at once the nation could have been successfully decapitated.

Walking up behind him Colonel Stamper

interrupted his musings and said, "General how bad is it?"

Turning to face his old friend he marveled at how young Stamper looked and he thought of all the tough situations they had faced together through the years. In Iraq and Afghanistan they had spent countless hours strategizing and planning everything from Covert Ops to massive campaigns, and today General Callaway knew they faced the gravest threat to their nation since either of them had put on the uniform back in the 80s.

"Rick, it's as bad as it can get. The White House and the Pentagon have both gone dark. I can't raise either of them. We can't raise either civilian or military command anywhere near Washington, even on private lines."

"Do we have any birds in the air? What do the satellites show?" asked Colonel Stamper.

"We should've visuals any minute, but from all the chatter and from reports coming in it looks like there're terrorist attacks taking place in at least three states besides DC. There are reports from State police of massive troop movements, and it seems that the terrorist have taken over several towns all of them the home of a National Guard Armored Brigade," answered the General as he waited for the images that would tell him so much more of what they needed to know.

Just then the sergeant in charge of the communications room said, "General, Captain Simmons reports that you are needed in the Staff Meeting Room."

Without a word General Callaway turned, and with Colonel Stamper right beside him made his way to the Staff Meeting Room where he was greeted by his gathering command staff. "Let's see what has happened."

On the long mahogany table satellite pictures were spread out showing a massive cloud of smoke following the wind east from Washington, DC. Infrared photos showed flames where the White House, Congress, the Pentagon and several other legendary locations had once stood. Other photos showed huge fires in Richmond, Baltimore, and Harrisburg. Still more showed heavy black smoke streaming away from the four towns surrounding DC that housed four of the best equipped Armored Brigades in America's National Guard.

"What about the AWACS? Where's the intel from the AWACS?" General Callaway·asked as he looked intently at the High Def pictures on the table.

"The Air Force says they are still twenty minutes out," responded Simmons.

"Is there any response from the Governors?"

"No sir."

"Contact the Commanding Generals of every National Guard in the Division and tell them I'm nationalizing them immediately and that they're to mobilize and prepare to march on Washington as soon as they have boots on the ground. And tell them I want them all to report to me here for central planning and execution."

"Yes sir!" Simmons said as he left the room to convey the General's orders.

"It looks like we are not only facing at least four armored brigades they're our own brigades and the four closest to Washington. Jacobs I want you to find out exactly what the Guard has available within striking distance."

"Yes sir I'm on it," Major Ralph Jenkins, the Division's liaison to the Guard, responded while immediately leaving the room to gather the needed information.

"I want maps in here now!"

"Yes sir we have them right here," Lieutenant Jim Thompson answered as he walked into the room and began spreading maps out on the big table. In moments the group of officers was huddled over the maps and satellite photos.

Holding one infrared photo Colonel Stamper compared it to the big map of DC and said, "General it looks like these Bastards are dug in at four major hospitals."

"Let me see that," the General said holding out his hand. Looking from the picture to the map he continued, "You're right Rick. The heat signatures of all those Army vehicles are unmistakable."

Just then Captain Simmons came in followed by Major Jenkins, "Sir the Governors of Virginia, Maryland, and Pennsylvania are all saying that only the president can nationalize the guard and that they are mobilizing to respond to attacks in their own States," Major Jenkins said.

Captain Simmons added, "The AWACS are in the air and they're starting to report."

"Pipe it in," the General said as he thought

about the information Jenkins had reported.

"Jenkins what about the other States?"

"All the other states are responding. They're mobilizing and their Commanding Generals are on their way," Jenkins answered.

"This is AWAC Delta One," came a voice from the overhead speakers.

"Delta One what kind of chatter are you picking up from the enemy formations in Washington?" asked the General as he began looking at a new batch of satellite photos a sergeant had just brought in and set on the table.

"We aren't hearing anything. There's no electronic communication going on between the four locations, and we aren't picking up anything inside the four locations."

"Nothing?"

"Yes sir, they're completely dark as far as electronic communication, at least in any frequency we can monitor," responded the voice from the AWAC.

"That doesn't make any sense," interjected Colonel Stamper, "they've got to be communicating somehow."

"Maybe they're using runners or some new frequency we don't know about," Lieutenant Thompson offered.

"We can monitor all possible radio frequencies and there's nothing," came the voice of the AWAC.

"What about walkie-talkies or cell phones?" asked the General.

"Some walkie-talkies may be so low tech we aren't equipped to pick them up and cell phones are restricted by policy," replied the voice from the speakers.

"Policy be damned! You listen into any cell traffic coming from those four sites or anything else going on in there," snapped General Callaway.

"Yes sir!"

Pointing to one of the newest satellite photos Stamper said, "From the heat signatures it looks like there's small arms fire punctuated by artillery going on at the perimeters of all four sites."

"From the look of it the artillery is all coming from the enemy," Lieutenant Thompson added.

"You're right," Stamper responded, "See the

flash of fire here and the explosion of impact here," he continued pointing at flashes on two separate photos. "It looks like the enemy positions are taking fire from the outside."

"At least someone is moving on these terrorists keeping them pinned down till we can get some troops on the scene," the General said as he too looked at the photos.

"Sir we aren't picking up any cell use between or within the four locations except for civilians who are obviously sheltering in place and haven't been rounded up by the terrorists," said the disembodied voice from the ceiling.

"What're they saying?" asked the General.

"Most are describing masses of uniformed men, heavily armed, who're speaking Arabic. They're describing mass casualties and that the intruders are killing all the male staff except for doctors and they're rounding up all the female staff and herding them off somewhere. The patients are being left where they are if they're bed bound. There are many reporting that the assailants are executing any of the patients that are ambulatory."

"Those lousy sons-a-bitches!" Lieutenant Thompson said under his breath.

"Simmons have communications raise the Washington PD and pipe them in as soon as you reach their command" ordered the General.

"Yes sir," Captain Simmons said as he used his cell phone to relay the orders to the Division Communications Room.

In the midst of all this hectic but well-ordered chaos of command, Stage Three of the attack came crashing in like another ton of bricks.

Captain Simmons looked up from his phone conversation with the communications room and said, "Sir reports are pouring in from the whole DC area, all the way to Baltimore, Richmond, and Harrisburg that snipers are taking out motorists especially tanker trucks up and down the expressways, bridges on the interstates are being blown, sniper and mortar fire also has the Washington PD headquarters tied down. RPGs fired from rooftops right into their main conference office have taken out the chief and her whole staff. Also, hospitals throughout the region have come under attack."

A stunned silence gripped the room broken by Lieutenant Colonel Sue Hack the Division Intelligence Officer, "This is unbelievable."

"This may be beyond belief and the impossible may take a little longer but we're going to hit these fools so hard they're going to wake up in heaven and tell their seventy-two virgins they wish they would have stayed in bed," the General said.

Turning to Colonel Stamper the General said, "Rick I want you to go down there and personally take command of every troop we can bring to bear. I want you to stomp these Jihadi pot lickers until there's nothing left but an oil slick."

"Yes sir! I'm on my......." Was all Stamper got out as four mortar rounds landed on the headquarters building quickly followed by four more and then four more while at the same time small arms fire broke out from dozens of buildings around the perimeter of Fort Hamilton. War had come to Brooklyn as the Caliphate's stage three brought most of America's immediate coordinated military response to a blazing halt.

CHAPTER TEN

Where There's Smoke There's Fire

Lisa Edwards, a nine year veteran of the Washington Fire Department, rolled over in her bunk at the new Firehouse 27 on Southern Avenue SE. She was the first female member of Truck 27, and it had taken her two years to break through the good-old-boys network until now with five years on the truck and a proven record as a solid firefighter the other members of the team were comfortable with her. They knew she could hold up her end of the ladder, and if they needed help she would have their backs. She was comfortable too, especially now that there were a few more women at the house.

With twelve years as an Air Force Fire and Rescue specialist who served time in Iraq and Afghanistan Lisa thought she was prepared for anything. Her husband of four years had recently left with a woman who looked like a younger version of herself. She was living alone for the first time in her life, and she didn't really like it. There was no one to say good night to, and no one to hear a good morning from. She recently began going to bars. At first just for the company of other people at night, and lately because she was in to getting drunk, and she discovered she liked the company of younger men.

Today was her second day back on shift, and she felt like she was still wearing off a hangover. As she rolled over in the bed, not quite ready to get up and start the day she was glad that at least her head wasn't pounding. It was only a dull ache. "I had too much Tequila. It always gives me a two day condition," she thought as she snuggled deeper under the covers and fluffed her pillow for the third time. She stretched and scratched her leg as she thought about Brad the boy-toy she had taken home the night before. He was only twenty-four and she rolled over again as she thought, "That boy may have been as dumb as a box of rocks but he certainly had some go power." She was still smiling thinking of Brad when the house klaxon horn split the silence and interrupted reliving in her mind what a hardy young man he was.

She had heard the klaxon more times than she could remember, but this morning instead of announcing where the fire was it was followed by an announcement, "All hands on deck! Report to the Ready Room immediately."

Just like every other fireman for generations she was up and dressed as quickly as humanly possible, and within a few moments she was walking with the rest of the crew into the Ready Room.

"All right everyone take a seat," barked Captain Rodriquez the Battalion Chief of House 27.

The scraping of chairs and the general muttering about a new situation was followed by the Chief bellowing, "Sit down and shut up! We don't have time for everyone to play twenty questions or ten complaints. So listen up!" Coming from the usually very polite and encouraging Rodriquez this caught everyone's attention. Suddenly you could hear a pin drop as everyone waited to see what this was all about.

"This is it. This is the day we've dreaded and the day we've been training for. Terrorists have attacked the DC metro area."

The quiet exploded into shouts and groans, "What the hell!" "Where" "How many casualties?" joined curses and sighs as the stunned team vented their anger, fear, and

Dr. Robert Owens

anxiety.

"Hold it down! Hold it down!" soothed Rodriquez "We don't have time for all this drama bullshit."

Quiet snapped over the room like a cap on a bottle and into the expectant stillness the Captain said, "There're multiple attacks and they're still going on." Then pausing because he couldn't believe he was about to say what needed to be said, "The White House, the Capital, and the Supreme Court have all been hit."

"Oh my God!" "How bad is it?" "Is the President safe?" "Who are they?" "Kill the bastards!" were just some of the epithets, questions, and exclamations that filled the air generously mixed with sobs, shouts, and stunned silence.

"There's no word on casualties at any of these sites but it doesn't sound good," Rodriquez shouted over the din. "The terrorists have also seized four major hospitals and attacked the Police Headquarters. There're fire fights going on around all of these sites as police try to assault the terrorists, but they are dug in and extremely well-armed."

"What can we do?" "Let's go" "Come on let's

64

roll" the shouts filled the room as the shocked first responders were eager to help.

"One of the hospitals the terrorists have seized is St. Elizabeth's, and there're multiple fires all around the area and as I said small arms fire from all sides. But that isn't all. From what I've been told the terrorists have tanks and other armored vehicles dug in around the perimeter of the hospital, the fence line has been reinforced with cement barricades and other obstacles, and there are enemy snipers scattered throughout the neighborhoods in every direction."

"Will we have any police cover?" asked Lieutenant Williams the commander of truck 27.

"As I said there're police and even some civilians firing from all directions assaulting the facilities. There won't be any direct police cover, not like we're used to in dangerous situations. Everything's just too chaotic" Rodriquez answered. "Let's mount up. We'll survey the situation when we get there and do whatever we can. Stay safe, and God be with us all."

Moving from the Ready Room to the vehicles that comprised the full complement of Fire

House 27 showed how this dedicated group of professionals could operate as a well-oiled machine, a team that through training and experience was as good as it gets. In moments with the Battalion Chief in the lead followed by Truck 27, Ladder Truck 27-A, Squad Truck 27, and two ambulances were racing southeast of Southern Avenue SE. Soon they were making the turn onto Wheeler Road SE with all sirens screaming and everyone tense as they hurtled headlong into their first active terrorist situation.

They turned off Alabama Avenue SE onto Dogwood Street and were almost opposite the Congress Heights Metro Station when a sniper's bullet slammed into the left temple of Captain Roberto Rodriquez. The twenty-five year veteran of the Washington DC Fire Department, devoted husband, and father of four slumped over the wheel. His command car swerved into a line of parked cars blocking the road.

All the trucks came to a screeching halt. Lieutenant Williams jumped out of the squad truck and started towards the Chief's car. He hadn't taken more than four steps when a bullet ripped through his face. He crumpled like a marionette whose strings had been cut as the back of his head exploded in a spray of blood and brains. In quick succession bullets found the gas tank of the command car causing it to explode into a fireball that engulfed the nearest parked cars and created a complete blockade as tight as the Boulder Dam on the Colorado.

The firemen were all jumping out of their trucks and pulling off what they needed to fight the fire. While some were hooking up the hoses to the trucks others were pulling out the hoses and rushing towards the flames as the gas tanks of some of the other cars started to explode with deafening crashes and shock waves that knocked down anyone in their path. While the men and women of Fire House 27 were trying to get to their Chief's car to clear a path to the unfolding emergency the sniper continued to rain death into their ranks. Bullet after bullet found its mark and one after another dropped into pools of blood as the fires raged and the explosions shattered windows and eardrums.

Lisa was in the rear compartment of truck 27 and on the opposite side from the shooter. She was running towards the front to grab onto a hose being pulled out when just as she broke into the clear the man in front of her,

Eddy Bailey, one of the most diehard good-old-boys she had to deal with when she first arrived and one of her best friends now, keeled over as the right side of his face disintegrated in blood and gore. Lisa's momentum caused her to trip over his body which was the only thing that saved her from the next bullet which instead went across the street and hit a twelve year old girl who was looking out her window trying to see what was going on.

As Lisa was trying to get up, Jamie Matheson, her best friend at the house and mother of her godchild, fell on top of her. Lisa grabbed Jamie and dragged her back behind the truck, "Jamie! Jamie look at me, look at me!" Lisa shouted as Jamie's eyes flickered for a brief second with life before glazing over in the blank stare of death Lisa had seen so many times during her deployments.

For what seemed like an eternity but was really only seconds Lisa held the lifeless body of her friend as tears slid down her cheeks. Then another firefighter, Bill Jeffords, a crusty old veteran of thirty-five years whose retirement party was scheduled for next Friday, staggered back from the front of the truck and collapsed on top of the grieving Lisa.

As death and destruction flew in small lead

projectiles and as cars burned and people died something snapped in Lisa. During her deployments she had carried a weapon as all the firemen in combat areas do. She had even been in a couple of firefights and though she couldn't be sure since they didn't do body counts as they did in Vietnam she was sure she had killed and wounded more people than she had ever wanted to think about. She had been trained and she had experience, but that day none of it figured into her thoughts because she wasn't thinking she was reacting. She was reacting to the situation, reacting to her fear, and most of all reacting to the death of her best friend as she shouted, "Let's get this son-of-a-bitch."

She pushed Tim off her, gently laid Jamie on the ground, and climbed to her feet. She could hear bullets smacking into the other side of the truck. The black oil and rubber smoke from the burning vehicles stunk to high heaven and made her eyes water as she grabbed up a fire ax from the hands of a fallen friend and headed for the back of the truck.

Followed by two others, Jimmy Dorsey and Sharon Wells, the three firefighters could see that the shooter was in the Metro Station. They crouched behind cars. Lisa led the way down the block until she thought she might be out of his immediate line of site as he continued to rain bullets down on the stalled column of emergency vehicles.

Staying low but running fast they crossed the side yard of the station and crouched behind the brick wall next to a side door. Once she caught her breath Lisa eased up and peered through the window into the waiting room. There wasn't just one there were two men in American military fatigues with AR-15s firing through a window on the other side. Lisa slid back down and said, "I'll take the one on the right. You two take the one on the left." She was the only one with anything that might be called a weapon. The other two just had their hands which were itching to get around the throat of the man who was killing their friends and coworkers.

Without saying another word Lisa slowly and as quietly as possible opened the door. As they entered they tried to move quietly and quickly, and though they were quick they weren't all that quiet. The sound of the rifle fire masked their advance until they were almost on top of the two terrorists. Then the one on the left looked over his shoulder shouting something in Arabic. Both men started to turn, but before they could bring their guns to bear the firefighters were on top of them. Lisa smashed the ax down on the exposed neck of the shooter on the right. He immediately fell with a groan as blood spurted from severed arteries.   On her left her two companions jumped the other man. With all the adrenalin pumping force he could muster Jimmy grabbed the gun with one hand while he punched the man in the face. Sharon hit him low and took his legs out from under him. All three fell in a squirming and shouting heap.

The terrorist, a veteran of many battles, a dedicated ISIS warrior committed to giving his life for the true faith, and the father of three children who had all been killed by Assad's barrel bombs shouted "Alah Akbar" as he let go of his gun, pulled a knife, and plunged it into Jimmy's exposed stomach. Jimmy let out a loud wail and let go of the man who was now free to turn his attention to Sharon. He grabbed her by the hair and was just about to slit her throat when a shot rang out and he slumped over dead.

Lisa stood over him rifle in hand and kicked the knife his lifeless hand had dropped away from the body as Sharon crawled out from underneath.

Looking out the widow that was just moments before the portal for death and destruction, Lisa could see other firefighters rushing towards the station now that the firing had stopped. She saw others finally able to get water and fire extinguishers on the scene of the fires, and she knew soon they would have the situation under control. She also saw people in the neighborhood coming out of their homes now that the shooting had stopped.

The first through the door was Lieutenant Gary Edmonson the commander of Squad 27 followed by several others from his elite team. "Good work Lisa and you too Sharon. See to Jimmy," Gary said to his team as he surveyed the room.

Lisa also looked around for the first time and noticed that the place was strewn with the bodies of early commuters who thought they were safe in a quiet residential neighborhood on the right side of the tracks in the capital of the greatest power the world had ever known.

As if her hearing had been turned off and with her ears still ringing from the concussions of the exploding cars, all of a sudden she was aware of the almost constant sound of small arms fire up ahead in the direction of the Hospital. She kicked the fallen gun towards the Lieutenant and said, "Better pick that up. I don't think we've seen the last of these murdering assholes yet."

Two of his men were carrying Jimmy out the door as Gary picked up the weapon. He was a retired marine who knew how to handle a gun and knew how to kill the enemy. "Lisa, you and I'll provide cover for the company. Stay here. I'll go to the other side of the street so we can cover more than one approach."

"Yes sir," Lisa snapped as she reverted to her former military self and took a place crouching behind the wall peering out the same window which just a short time before had threatened the firefighters but was now their sentinel: their cover as they hurriedly worked to put out the fires and clear a path to the hospital.

CHAPTER ELEVEN

When Duty Calls

David Johnson first joined the West Virginia National Guard when he was a junior in high school. He spent the summer between his junior and senior years in boot camp. Then he had used the college benefits to complete his bachelor's degree while rising through the ranks of the ROTC. By the time he graduated he was the student commander of his squad.

After graduation he went into the regular army as a second lieutenant in the infantry. After eight years of service he rose to the rank of captain in the 38th Armored Division commanding Company A for the 4th Brigade, which was made up of two hundred fifty men, three tank platoons of four Abrams tanks, a headquarters with two Abrams tanks, a

M113A2 armored personnel carrier, two M998
HMMWV's, and two 2.5-ton trucks with trailers.

Like everyone else in America he was shocked
by the attacks of 9-11, which happened during
his first four year hitch. He volunteered for
deployment five times serving three tours in
Afghanistan and two in Iraq. He had earned
two bronze stars and was wounded by a sniper
on his final deployment in Ramadi.

In 2008 at thirty years old he transitioned out
of the regular army but he stayed in the guard
intending to serve until he could retire. Almost
as soon as he was out he was snapped up by
the West Virginia State Police. Now after eight
years on the force he was a patrol sergeant
who just passed his Lieutenant's test and
recently recruited to join the State's Detective
Squad at the end of the month. After eight
years in the guard he was now a full colonel,
and he was in command of the 13th Armored
Brigade with its headquarters as the Charles
Town Armory.

That morning he was having breakfast with his
childhood sweetheart who was now his wife of
fifteen years. They were talking about the
vacation they were planning for the coming
summer.

"I just can't wait to see the Rocky Mountains," said Tammy.

"Me too I want to see how they match up to the Alps."

The time they spent in Bavaria when he was stationed outside of Munich had been their favorite duty post. Being from the mountains they felt most at home when the horizon was cut off by rising peaks and the mornings were filled with misty pinks and purples as cold water streams skipped over tumbles and jumbles of rocks. The Alps had shown them that their home mountains in the Blue Ridge were small and friendly compared with the big rock mountains of the world. For two years they had been planning for a whole month of hiking and climbing in the Colorado Rockies.

"I wish Johnny could come with but that soccer camp is going to be great for him, and it should help him make first string next year," David said as he poured another cup of coffee. Their only son Johnny was working hard to earn a soccer scholarship and both of them knew he needed the help a concentrated month long camp would give him. They both regretted that the only spot he could get in the camp was the same month as David's vacation.

"When do you think you'll be home tonight," Tammy asked, "the Farrells want to have dinner by seven."

"That should be no problem as long as the good Lord's willing and the crick don't rise," answered David with a smile.

"I hope Jim isn't going to want to talk about nothing but the Mountaineers and whether or not they'll make it to the playoffs," Tammy said as she cut a second piece of her locally famous Aronia and Cinnamon Crunch coffee cake for the love of her life.

"I hope Jenny is making those pork fritters again," responded David as he eagerly pushed his fork into the coffee cake.

Then David's phone rang and their lives would never be the same.

"Colonel Johnson."

Recognizing the voice of General James "Crash" Corbaine, the Commanding General of the West Virginia National Guard and an old friend David answered, "Yes sir."

"David I need you to get to the armory immediately. The Governor has ordered full mobilization. Your men should be arriving in short order. I need you to mount up every vehicle you have for immediate deployment to Washington DC."

Startled by the unusual order David asked, "What's up General? Somebody in DC need an emergency parade?"

"This is no joke David, and it isn't a drill. The capital has been hit and hit hard and we need to get there as fast as we can."

"I'm on my way sir and the 13th will be on the road ASAP."

"I knew I could count on you. I'll give you more details and specific deployment orders once you get in the saddle and we have a secure line."

David kissed his wife goodbye telling her, "I love you," as he quickly changed from his trooper's uniform into his fatigues. He took his patrol car because with sirens wailing and a 460 eliminator engine he was able to make better time on his way to the armory. It took him a little less than thirty minutes to cover the twenty miles. He listened to the police radio all the way. It was filled with reports of massive terrorist attacks in DC and with orders for all personnel to report for duty.

When he came to the gate the sergeant of the guard saluted him while raising the gate in front of him and lowering it quickly behind him. A moment later he was climbing out of his prowler as his second-in-command, Lt. Colonel Bobby Larson, met him followed by the rest of the brigade staff officers.

The yard was filled with men busy fueling vehicles and firing up tanks, Bradleys and the other vehicles of the brigade. "How's the muster so far?" David asked as he slammed the door of his car and started into the huge old brick building that dated from World War One.

"Of course the local boys are here already and so far we have less than a dozen troops who have said they can't make it," Larson said as he fell in behind his commanding officer and lifetime friend.

The roar of diesels and the smell of fuel permeated the air in the building just as it had in the massive yard that was one big parking lot for the 13th. David walked into his office just as the phone rang. His adjutant, First Sergeant Billy "Bubba" Hanks picked up the phone and answered, "13th Armored Brigade, Colonel Johnson's office."

David sat down behind the battered old desk that had been used by the commanders of this armory since 1918. Sergeant Hanks handed the phone to the Colonel saying "Sir, it's General Corbaine."

"Johnson here."

"David this is bad. Four armories were taken by terrorist during the night. Each one was the home of an armored brigade. They were able to mobilize and move into DC before anyone knew what was happening. Right now they're occupying four major hospitals, and they're spreading death and destruction in every direction."

"Oh my God!"

"David, that isn't even the worst of it. The White House, Congress, and the Pentagon all have been hit. The civilian and military chains of command are MIA. The Governors of Virginia, Pennsylvania, and Maryland are refusing to nationalize their Guards because their States are also under terrorist attack. I've just been told that Fort Hamilton is under attack and that General Callaway and his whole staff can't be reached."

"Oh Lord this is a full blown invasion. Where did they come from? How did they get here?"

"I don't have any answers David all I know is we've got a shooting war right here, and we have got to start doing some shooting. I want you to take the 13th down 340 to I-270. One of the enemy brigades is dug in at Walter Reed. I'll send the 24th and the 11th to your location ASAP. I want you to command the Division. David they have a heavy brigade, Apache cover, the whole nine-yards. Keep your head down and clean these creeps out of our hospital."

Colonel Johnson was not the senior officer out of the three brigade commanders being sent to Walter Reed but he had the most combat experience and General Corbaine had been pushing for his promotion to brigadier for quite a while. Out of all the officers in the West Virginia Guard if there was one man the general wanted at the tip of the spear it was David.

"Yes sir we should be pulling out in a few minutes."

"David I am just now receiving reports that there are snipers hitting commuters on I-270, and at least one bridge has been blown."

"The 13th will get through General."

"I know you will David, I know you will."

Turning to Colonel Larson David said, "Colonel let's get these men rolling." Forty minutes later as the sun was breaking over the horizon spreading pinks and reds over clouds that seemed to be waiting for just such illumination the 13th Armored Brigade of the West Virginia National Guard was rolling down 340. David was in the lead Humvee, and he was getting reports of multiple sniper hits on I-270.

Opening a secure channel to the entire convoy David said, "Men as you have been briefed we're heading into battle. It looks like we're going to encounter some snipers on the way. If we take any fire I want the lead Bradley to follow the fire and take it out. There're also reports of at least one bridge down on the road. When we come to it I want a Bradley screen to clear the area, and then I want the sappers to clear the debris. We're on our way to liberate Walter Reed, and no one I repeat no one is going to stop us."

Moving at top speed the convoy soon reached the junction with I-270. They saw evidence of sniper activity in numerous crashed vehicles, some burning and others off the road. Traffic was mostly pulled off the road. A few cars were either smoking or burning, and ambulances and police were on the scene.

The convoy didn't stop. It rolled onto I-270 and was soon once again up to top speed.

Just north of Gaithersburg they took their first fire. The driver of a fuel tanker was hit and he slumped over the wheel. The man riding shotgun tried valiantly to grab the wheel and stop the truck but he couldn't with the dead man's foot still on the gas the semi plunged off the road and hit a bridge abutment exploding and bursting into flames with a deafening roar.

The fuel truck was in the middle of the convoy, so they were now cut in two as snipers opened up from multiple locations. Knowing they didn't have armored glass like the Humvees and the Bradleys the expert marksman aimed at the drivers of the trucks. Soon numerous trucks were off the road, some smoking, some on fire, and all filled with injured and dead troopers.

Following David's earlier orders Bradleys were splitting off and following the fire, mostly in trees and behind any cover they could find. The Bradleys using their 25 MM guns which can fire up to two hundred rounds per minute made short work of the snipers. After using two Bradleys to push the still burning tanker out of the way the convoy was soon rolling again determined to take death and destruction to the invaders.

Just south of Rockville they were hit by snipers again. Following the same pattern the snipers picked out truck drivers as easy targets. This time there were only two. No drivers were killed, and the convoy rolled on with Bradleys taking out the snipers on the fly. Within two and a half hours of receiving the call at his home in Charlestown, Colonel Johnson and the 13th were rolling across the beltway and nearing the Walter Reed hospital complex in Bethesda.

CHAPTER TWELVE

The Grey Ghost Wears Fatigues

Just like any other morning Mitch Williams was busy opening up his gun shop in Dinwiddie, Virginia. He always arrived at 6 AM, turned off the security system, tuned on the coffee and the lights as he put the cash in the register and then settled down in his office to scan the headlines on the Drudge Report, listen to talk radio, and have his first cup of coffee.

If that day had been like any other he would have spent the next two hours drinking a few cups of coffee heavy on the flavored creamers and having a piece, maybe even two, of the tasty apple cinnamon crisp his wife had sent with him. But this morning wasn't like any other day. This was the day he had been waiting for, the day he had predicted would come, the day he dreaded above all others.

Both Drudge and the newscaster on WRVA jarred him out of the life he had lived for forty-seven years and into a new world where nothing would ever be the same again.

"Fires are raging in downtown Richmond. Eye witnesses tell us that just after sunrise a large jet crashed into the VCU Medical Center. The resulting explosions and fire have engulfed most of the VCU campus. When the first fire trucks and police arrived on the scene they were attacked by multiple snipers. In light of the massive attack now underway in Washington, DC it is obvious that America is under attack," reported the obviously shaken radio newsman. The headline on Drudge shouted, "DC Under Attack" in bright red.

Swiveling around in his big leather office chair Mitch was facing the large ham radio that he used to keep up on international news and to communicate with his well-developed Network of Patriot Militias. Mitch Williams was not just a successful entrepreneur and he was not just a loving husband and father of five. He was also the founder and commander of the Dinwiddie Patriots.

They were a local militia that had first begun to

develop as an offshoot of the Virginia Tea Party Movement back in 2011. They formed after the first Tea Party majority in the House of Representatives made it to Washington, and after they promptly re-elected Speaker of the House Jim Bowner, the leader of the RINOs, and then went on to pass continuing resolutions to fund the Obonyo agenda, renew the Patriot Act, and in general blend right into the problems they were elected to solve.

All over the country as reality sunk in after the betrayal of the 2010 Tea Party class in Congress groups spontaneously began forming all over the country. The Dinwiddie Patriots were comprised of over two hundred men and women, mostly veterans and many with combat experience. There was also a strong contingent of retired first responders. They were well organized and due to what they saw as the increasingly repressive and anti-constitutional nature of the Obonyo administration they were also underground. But they were neither unique nor alone. Mitch not only founded the Dinwiddie group he also led the way in forging the Virginia Patriot Network, an umbrella group that by 2016 incorporated more than one hundred units all over Virginia totaling more than two thousand members.

Listening in to the conversations going on amongst the many different groups Mitch soon knew that the Governor had decided not to nationalize the guard as requested by military officials. The consensus among the groups quickly grew that the attack in Richmond and others they were hearing about in Baltimore and up in Pennsylvania were all diversionary attacks and the real threat was in Washington. Though it wasn't being publicly reported it was all over the Patriot network that the White House and the Pentagon had both been obliterated.

By 7 AM the commanders of the many groups had made the decision that the Network needed to fully mobilize and head for DC.

This was the first time the groups had fully mobilized. They had run several drills where members assembled in different areas. It was hard to do and still remain under the radar, but they had figured it out by meeting in public places when large crowds were already expected. They had of course never brought their weapons or other equipment. They knew this action would compromise the secrecy and that it might even expose them to opposition or arrest by the government. All of that was outweighed by the gravity of this violent assault on the very center of American life.

Mitch sent a text to his wife and his two oldest sons who were all members of the Patriots. The two word text, "Let's Roll" went not only to Mitch's family but to everyone in the group. Soon several members including his family were at the gun shop loading weapons and ammunition in to a line of vehicles that had materialized as if by magic in response to Mitch's text.

The Dinwiddie group, as with most of the groups, had been training and drilling for just such a situation for years on a large farm in rural Virginia that had been in Mitch's family for hundreds of years. Surrounded by woods they had carried out live fire drills and tactical briefings always in secret and always in anticipation of either a move by the government to impose martial law, a breakdown in society, or a foreign invasion. Most feared the first two scenarios and dismissed the last as too farfetched, but Mitch had always made sure it was included in the planning.

By 8 AM the Dinwiddie Patriots like hundreds of other Patriot groups were traveling north in small groups to avoid detection or interference. The leadership of the Network had decided that since the military in America was in many ways disarmed and scattered, and since the Virginia National Guard was mobilizing and heading to Richmond they would converge on Arlington and take back the Virginia Hospital Center.

They had no idea what they were going to encounter from the enemy. They couldn't count on support from the first responders. They were all quite sure that if the current Administration survived they would probably be prosecuted. But at the same time they also knew they weren't going to stand idly by while terrorists were occupying even one square inch of the Old Dominion. Into the emerging day these descendants of the Army of Northern Virginia, these genetic and spiritual descendants of the Grey Ghost and his irregulars, moved out of obscurity and into the blinding light of their date with destiny.

CHAPTER THIRTEEN

A Phoenix Rising From the Ashes

Battered but not broken the remnants of General Callaway's staff began to recover consciousness after the last salvo of mortar shells exploded into ripping shrapnel maiming and killing its way through the Command Center of the North Atlantic Military Division.

The mortar squad was made up of twelve men. They consisted of three homegrown terrorists radicalized on the Internet, two gang members who converted to Islam while in Atica, and four sleeper cell members two cab drivers, a dishwasher, and a loner living on welfare. They were spotted almost immediately by a neighborhood radio car. They killed the two officers in the car, but not before they could get off an alert to their precinct. Consequently they managed to get off only four salvos before they were overwhelmed by cars full of New York's finest arriving from all locations.

The snipers who were surrounding Fort Hamilton were soon hunted down and eliminated. They killed almost a dozen police officers and civilians, but in the end the first responders took them out.

While these firefights were raging around the perimeter of the Fort, Colonel Stamper regained his feet. Surveying the scene he knew immediately that General Callaway was dead. The unnatural tilt to his head and the severe gash in the side of his neck told Stamper that his friend of thirty years was gone. Shoving aside a part of the broken top of the conference table Rick uncovered Lieutenant Jim Thompson. He was covered in dust and he wasn't moving, but the colonel didn't see any wounds or obvious broken bones so he gently nudged the lieutenant with his boot, "Jim are you alive?'

Coughing and sputtering Thompson rolled to one side and asked, "What happened?"

"From the sounds they made when the secondary salvos came in I'd say we got hit with mortar fire."

"How's the General? Is he all right?"

"He didn't make it," said Stamper as he began to dig around in the debris looking for other survivors. Members of the Fort's fire department were pushing their way into the ruins of the big conference room. Fire extinguishers in hand they were putting out small fires as EMTs worked feverishly to save some as they methodically moved from body to body leaving the dead for later as they raced to treat the living.

As the senior man on sight Colonel Stamper took command.

Walking into the communications room Stamper asked, "Have you been able to raise the Pentagon?"

"No sir, there's no response on any frequency and the phones are down too," answered Master Sergeant Luke Welling.

"Keep trying, and have one of your men get me Admiral Downs at Hampton Roads."

"Yes Sir."

As Stamper walked out of the communications room he was glad to see Major Jenkins coming towards him. Jenkins had one arm in a sling, his uniform was torn, and blood was oozing through a bandage around his head and starting to drip down onto his left shoulder.

"Ralph, are you all right? You look like you should go to the hospital."

"I'm fit for duty sir, and I'm not going anywhere until we start landing some punches on these guys."

"All right," Stamper said. He had known Major Jenkins since his second tour in Iraq when he had joined General Callaway's staff as a newly minted Lieutenant fresh out of West Point. He knew he was a talented leader and a determined and dedicated soldier.

Stamper walked down the hall to his office with Major Jenkins in tow. "Close the door Ralph," Rick said as he took a seat on the edge of his desk. Jenkins closed the door and sat down in one of the two brown leather wing backed chairs facing Stamper's desk.

"Look Ralph this is a full blown assault. These guys have caught us with our pants down. They've taken out command and control in DC. They were well armed and well organized enough to coordinate an attack on us at the same time and from reports coming in there are attacks going on across the country and around the world. We've no idea who is in command either in the civilian or the military chain and we've got to make a move. We have to bring this battle to them and hit them hard."

"I agree with all of that Rick, so what are you suggesting we do?" Ralph asked.

"We have the best trained and best equipped Special Ops force in the Division right here and I'm sure after all this," he waved his hand to include all the death and destruction around them, "I'm sure my guys are suited up and ready to roll. So I'm going to take the Chinooks and Apaches and head for Washington. If I can convince Admiral Downs I'll have the Seal Teams from Hampton Roads rendezvous with us in DC. But with the Seals or without them we're going to take the fight to the enemy."

"Can I go with you," asked Major Jenkins even as the blood began to run down the side of his face.

"No Ralph, I want you to stay here and coordinate anything and everything you can. Try to get the governors to have their Guard units move on Washington ASAP, especially Virginia. They have units that haven't been compromised closer than anyone. And get the medics to bind up that head wound or you're going to lose so much blood you'll pass out."

Putting his hand to his head when he pulled it away, he saw the blood, "I'm all right Colonel. I'll get this taken care of and get on the horn with the Governor of Virginia."

Leaving the shattered headquarters building behind him Rick was relieved to see that he had been correct in his estimation of his Special Ops team. He knew he was prejudiced but he honestly believed they were the best trained and most capable Ranger quick response team in the Army. He had built the unit himself from the ground up hand-picking all the officers and non-coms who then hand-picked the troopers.

Numbering three hundred men they had been together through several full deployments in Iraq and Afghanistan and more insertion ops than he could remember. They were cool and efficient under fire and all of them were patriots willing to sacrifice their lives for their country.

Walking towards him as he exited the building was his second-in-command, Lt. Colonel Bill "Huffy" Smith, and the three captains of the team Captain Jim Grady, Company A; Captain Joe Kearnz, Company B; and Captain Mahmoud Sarraf of Company C. "What're your orders," Hufffy said as Colonel Stamper met them and continued walking towards the Special Ops compound.

"We're going to DC."

Only then did anyone ask, "What's going on?"

Answering the question Stamper said over his shoulder as he entered the compound which was a buzz with men preparing for battle, "DC is under attack Jim and we're the ones who are going to rain death and destruction on every last terrorist that comes in range," using the outfit's motto, "Let it Rain – Death and Destruction."

As the Colonel walked into his headquarters building he ordered, "Mahmoud, get the birds ready for full deployment ASAP. I want everything loaded: the Humvees and the Howitzers and all the amo we can carry and still get off the ground."

"Yes sir!" Captain Sarraf snapped as he wheeled back into the early morning to fulfill his duties as chief transportation officer.

"Joe make sure every troop has his full kit,

nothing left behind. This is going to be an assault on an entrenched enemy. We will need everything we've got."

"Yes sir!" Captain Kearnz said as he too split off to prepare for the battle.

As they walked down the hall to his office Stamper said, "Jim contact Major Helverson and tell him I want every Apache we have in the air for escort and make sure he has them fully fueled and armed."

Yes, Sir!" responded Captain Grady stepping into the communications room to transmit the orders to Major Helverson.

As they entered Stamper's office Colonel Smith asked, "What's the situation Rick."

"The terrorists, it looks like either Al-Qaeda or ISIS or maybe even a combination of the two, have taken some National Guard armories and punched their way into DC. They've taken the White House and the Pentagon out. They're very coordinated. They've taken out Fort McNair, the Police Headquarters, and many individual precincts. They have moved into four hospitals including Walter Reed. They are holding the patients and staffs hostage. They've got the best we have: Abrams, Bradleys, Howitzers, Strykers and they even have an Apache cap. At the same time there've been large planes flying into hospitals in neighboring states and snipers all over the place: roads, cities, even some smaller towns. And if that wasn't enough there are attacks against our bases, embassies, and other assets all over the world. It's a full blown attack Huffy. These Bastards are trying to take us down."

Overwhelmed by the sheer volume of what he had just been told Huffy was silent for a moment. Then he said, "How in the hell did these monsters ever get so many warriors right here, right in DC?"

"I think we may have paid to bring them in," said Rick as he thought about the way the administration had brow beaten everyone into a spiral of silence as they brought in thousands upon thousands of "refugees" from the Mideast both over and under the radar.

"Thousands and thousands of the same exact people they've been paying us to kill were brought in to drive cabs and wash dishes. How could that ever go wrong?" Huffy said as both men looked at each other like two men who are facing a raging monster their leaders told them wouldn't attack them if they would just let it out of its cage and try to pet it.

Both men just shook their heads in sorrow as they readied themselves to face the fact that "How could that ever go wrong," had gone very very wrong indeed.

CHAPTER FOURTEEN

Birds of a Feather

"The birds are away," was the confirmation Major Jenkins received as the twelve Chinooks and ten Apaches roared into the early morning sky. The people around Fort Hamilton were used to military helicopters coming and going, but they never heard the sound of such a large flight taking off at once. The sound rattled windows, caused many people to wake up, and others to rush to their windows to see what was going on. In moments they were gone heading south at top speed.

At 175 MPH Colonel Stamper estimated that it would take them about fifty minutes to cover the two hundred-thirty miles from Brooklyn to DC. As soon as they were in the air he told the Co-pilot, Lieutenant Ed Jackson, "Get Admiral

Downs in Hampton Roads on the horn. Tell his office Fort Hamilton has been attacked, General Callaway is dead, our entire Delta Team is in the air moving on Washington, and I want to coordinate our response."

Moments later the co-pilot said, "Colonel I have Admiral Downs on the line."

"Thanks Jackson. Admiral Downs this is Colonel Stamper commanding officer of the Delta Team for the North Atlantic Military Division."

"Colonel Stamper what's the situation on your end?"

"Sir just as we were assessing the situation Fort Hamilton was hit by repeated mortar barrages and sniper fire. General Callaway was killed. The terrorists on our perimeter were taken out by NYPD. I have mobilized our entire Delta Force, and we are moving on Washington right now with an Apache escort."

"What do you need from me?" asked Admiral Downs.

"Sir I'm calling to ask if you will dispatch every SEAL Team at your disposal to join us in an assault on the terrorists."

"I'm way ahead of you. The SEAL Teams are already in the air. I'll transmit the Com Codes to your communications officer so that you can coordinate."

"How many teams are you sending sir?" asked Stamper.

"We're sending four teams with all their equipment. They're coming in a dozen Super Stallions with Apache and Cobra escorts," responded Admiral Downs.

"Excellent! From the latest satellite and AWAC Intel the enemy is holding four hospitals, three in DC proper and one in Arlington. I propose that instead of splitting up we combine our forces and concentrate on one target at a time."

"That sounds like a good plan Rick I'll order my teams to coordinate with you. We have to remember they are holding all the patients and staffs of those hospitals as hostages."

"Have you heard anything about the President or anyone else in the government?" asked Colonel Stamper.

"It looks like a clean sweep. No one has been able to reach the President, the Vice President, or any of the others in the line of succession," answered Admiral Downs.

"And the Pentagon or the Joint Chiefs?"

"No luck there either. Did General Callaway get a chance to nationalize the Guard?" asked Admiral Downs.

"The governors of Virginia, Maryland, and Pennsylvania have refused to nationalize citing the lack of a presidential order and the need to contain terrorist attacks in their States. The Guards of the other States in the Division should be mobilizing now and getting ready to move" answered Rick.

As the flying column from Fort Hamilton neared Annapolis they rendezvoused with the Seal Teams in fourteen Super Stallions escorted by fifteen Apache and Cobra gunships. As they headed to DC at top speed they decided to concentrate their attack on the first location they would come to, the Adventist Hospital Complex in northeast DC.

The combined force was rushing on with a deafening roar when out of the sun two terrorist controlled Apaches launched hellfire missiles from forty miles away. "Incoming!" shouted the pilots or co-pilots of more than a dozen ships at once, as they furiously tried to launch electronic and conventional countermeasures while at the same time taking evasive maneuvers.

Almost all of the helicopters were successful but the incoming missiles hit the lead SEAL Super Stallion taking out Commander Miles Nelson and his entire headquarters' staff. Two Ranger Chinooks were also hit. The explosions from these three sent shrapnel into four others: three SEAL Super Stallions and one Delta Force Chinook. All four were now smoking and trying to make controlled landings. The Apaches and Cobras returned fire. The enemy Apaches were heading up and out at full speed. They deployed every countermeasure they could. Still the salvo of Hellfire missiles either connected or exploded close enough that the two enemy copters were soon heading to earth to crash in residential neighborhoods helping to spread death and destruction in the heart of America.

Not taking time to fly down to check on either the destroyed or the disabled copters the formation hurriedly regrouped and continued on towards DC.

It was now several hours after sunrise and several hours after the decapitation of the American political and military leadership. Relief columns were converging on three of the enemy held positions when deep within the bowls of Walter Reed Hospital Abdal El Shallab the Supreme Commander and the first Governor of the ISIS Province of America turned to his second in command and said, "Launch Stage Four."

Adnan Kaib using one of the game station consoles they were using for communication typed in "Muhammed Awakes" and many things happened simultaneously.

Every heavy weapon in all four captured positions sent one incendiary round followed by one high explosive round flying into the city. Suddenly there were 744 massive new fires burning throughout the metro area. Thousands died and thousands more were wounded and dying engulfed by flames and falling buildings. If the Washington PD and FD hadn't ever been previously overwhelmed they were now paralyzed even before the vast scope of the human tragedy which had been unleashed in seconds upon them was realized.

At the same time suicide bombers around the country in cities large and small walked into Malls, hospitals, police departments, and schools. The huge MS-13 gang joined in the attack with their tens of thousands of members taking to the streets attacking police and fire

fighters as they attempted to respond to the attacks. The cartels and the large numbers of recruits and trainees from the ISIS training camps in Northern Mexico that had overwhelmed the southern border were now making military assaults in San Diego, Tucson, White Sands, and San Antonio.
Simultaneously the perimeter of every military installation in America was attacked by snipers and suicide bombers.

The sounds of sirens could be heard from millions of American homes as war was brought home to all of the lower forty-eight States. Columns of smoke rose to blot out the sun and many people wondered if the sun was setting on the American dream as a nightmare from the depths of hell unfolded in their lives.

Back in Washington Adnan followed the reports on his game station console soon turned to Abdal El Shallab and said, "The streets of America are running red with the blood of the Unbelievers, their women and their children wail as they have made ours wail."

"Good, good. Now we must await the assault that will allow us all to find joy in martyrdom. Now is the time to live a life of glorious death for the Caliph and the praise of God!"

Shouts of "Allah Akbar! Allah Akbar!" filled the makeshift headquarters as everyone present knew that the assault upon America had just peaked and from here on out it would be a matter of inflicting as much pain, death and destruction, on the Americans while they marched into History as the greatest suicide attack of all time.

"Adnan, tell the men, today we die for the Caliph and for Allah" Abdal said.

Soon throughout the four hospitals Adnan's announcement had barely finished ringing off the walls when the desecrated facilities meant to heal and save rang with the shouts of "Allah Akbar! Allah Akbar!" from the throats of tens of thousands of dedicated followers of the prophet determined to meet him in paradise for the glory of God.

CHAPTER FIFTEEN

The President Takes Command

Each phase of the ISIS invasion had knocked America back on its heels.

Washington was ablaze. More than a thousand individual fires were raging. The White House was a smoking crater as where Congress, the Supreme Court, and the Pentagon. The civilian and military chain of command had been decapitated in a strike so devastating and targeted, so effectively executed it went far beyond any advanced planning, war game simulation, or contingency plan. America's ship of state was rudderless at the moment of greatest peril.

Every police station in Washington was under attack. Fort McNair, Andrews AFB, Bolling AFB, and every other military facility in the capital was burning and under attack. There had been nothing like it since General Ross and the Redcoats had burned the city during the War of 1812.

There were snipers and bridges down on all the approaches to the city as well as along many other major highways throughout the nation. There were major fires burning caused by large corporate planes used as missiles in Richmond, Baltimore, and Harrisburg. Hundreds of other cities had fires burning from smaller private planes crashing into hospitals. Suicide bombers had blown themselves up at malls and other crowded public places all over the country. Every military installation in the country was under attack by snipers and suicide bombers.

By the time the final phase of the assault was launched at 10 AM Eastern time the whole world was watching. Our NATO Allies did nothing. Later they would say they waited for America's leadership to invoke Article Five of the NATO Treaty, which says that an attack on one is an attack on all. Since immediately after the attack there was no clear American leadership this gave the Old World a convenient excuse to stand aloof from this sneak attack on the New. They would also point out that they were busy dealing with the effects of the attacks on American bases in every one of the member countries. They would of course later deliver massive bills for all their help.

Russia and China both watched events unfold making no move to help. They bided their time waiting to see if the United States led by an administration leading from behind would be able to rise to this challenge.

Snakes coil before they strike, and the bite of a poisonous snake can kill. However in a battle between a snake and an eagle only a fool would bet on the snake.

In the darkest hour of the darkest day in America's History while everyone else in the world wondered what America would do, in hearts from sea to shining sea from alabaster cities and purple mountains from amber fields and fruited plains Americans of every race and nationality knew what we would do. No matter how long it may take to overcome this premeditated invasion, the American people, in their righteous might, would win through to absolute victory.

Through the billowing smoke of thousands of fires a ray of light broke through. Over the sound of explosions and gunfire a message was broadcast from Arizona that began to bring clarity to a kaleidoscope of changing tones. At 11 AM Eastern time Patricia Parker, the recently confirmed but not yet sworn in Secretary of Education, announced that according to the Presidential Succession Act of 1947 as amended in 2006 she was taking command as the highest ranking surviving Cabinet Secretary.

She was the ex-governor of Arizona who had been appointed to the post by President Obonyo as a gesture of conciliation to the right wing in America. The president rarely consulted his cabinet instead running the government through his many czars and the regulatory agencies that really controlled everything. Mr. Obonyo knew that in his revolutionary administration, built along the lines of an Alinsky-style Community Organization, the post was mainly a ceremonial ribbon-cutting affair. As the election year began he wanted to have the appearance of governing from the middle so that he could help the Democrats hold onto the White House and solidify the fundamental changes he had built into the once constitutionally constrained federal government.

Now, in the midst of this unfolding battle everyone was glad that someone was taking the helm of the civilian government. Parker had the Chief Justice of the Arizona Supreme Court swear her in as the President of the United States. She immediately called up the Arizona National Guard and moved her office to Fort Huachuca.

Fort Huachuca, located in Cochise County, in southeast Arizona, about fifteen miles north of the border with Mexico, is the home of the U.S. Army Intelligence Center and the U.S. Army Network Enterprise Technology Command (NETCOM)/9th Army Signal Command. Fort Huachuca is also the headquarters of the Army Military Affiliate Radio System (MARS) and the Joint Interoperability Test Command (JITC) and the Electronic Proving Ground (EPG).

As soon as President Parker arrived at Fort Huachuca she moved fast to fill the vacuum left by the attack in Washington. Not caring a fig about seniority, rank, or tradition as soon as her helicopter landed and she was in the Command Center of the base she appointed General Edward Brown the Commander of the U.S. Army Intelligence Center as the new Chief of Staff of the Army and the Chairman of the Joint Chiefs. As a twenty-five year veteran and retired colonel with four combat deployments the new President was determined that as Commander-in-Chief she would take direct command of the military, but she knew she needed someone to fill the slot and handle the particulars.

Having been stationed at Fort Huachuca during her career she was intimately familiar with all its capabilities. "General Brown have MARS broadcast on all frequencies that we have a new president and that every military facility around the world should use all means necessary to secure their positions. Contact General Zchevinsky at Davis–Monthan Air Force Base and tell him I have just appointed him Chief of Staff of the Airforce. Contact the Ranking admiral in Hampton Roads and tell him he is now the Chief of Naval Operations. Contact the Commanding General at Parris Island and tell him he is now Commandant of the Marine Corps. Contact General Wilson of the Arizona National Guard and tell him he is now *Chief* of the National Guard Bureau."

Everyone in the room was glad to have someone take charge and the mood in the room swelled from confusion and doubt to certainty and determination. General Brown was on the phone contacting the new Joint

Chiefs when President Parker added, "And have the new appointments broadcast over MARS. Be sure to state that these new appointments supersede any previous appointments and they are effective immediately."

"Yes Ma'am," the General replied as he told his adjutant to get the head of the radio on the line as he continued to make the calls to the new military chiefs.

"I want satellite pictures and all intel right here," said the President pointing at the large conference table. Turning to her personal secretary, Mike Bender, she said, "Contact General Wilson and tell him to transmit an order under my authority as president nationalizing the entire National Guard. And have him order the National Guards of Virginia, Maryland, West Virginia, and Pennsylvania to converge on Washington and take all measures necessary to defeat the enemy and secure the capital."

"Yes Ma'am," Bender said as he picked up a phone to transmit the orders.

Leadership and direction returned to the American chain of command as the Battle of Washington blazed on the streets with patriots:

military, first responders, and private citizens riding to the sound of the guns. Without anyone in overall command often without the tools necessary to do the job like the Boys of Pointe du Hoc these enraged patriots did what they had to do to stand in the gap. ISIS may have scored a hit, but they were a long way from winning a battle.

CHAPTER SIXTEEN

A Family Affair

Mitch Williams met his future wife Joan when he was fifteen years old at a high school dance in the spring of their sophomore year. He fell in love at first sight. He spent the night dancing with her, then accompanied her home, and went in and told her father, "I'm going to marry your daughter." Her father promptly threw him out of the house and forbade Joan to ever see him again.

That didn't work. By the end of that summer they were going steady. By the end of their junior year they were engaged even though Mitch couldn't afford a ring. They didn't tell anyone. Within a few months of their graduation they were both eighteen and even though Joan's parents refused to attend they were married in a small ceremony at a little chapel in the woods.

Unable to find any work in rural Virginia Mitch joined the Army and for the next twenty-two years they moved all over the world. After qualifying for and finishing Officer Candidate School Mitch rose to the rank of Captain and served in the First Gulf War before he retired and returned home to Dinwiddie to open his gun store.

Theirs was a love story that never seemed to grow old. Though now in their late forties Mitch often told friends he "Had the best wife in the world." When asked how long they had been married his answer was always, "Not long enough."

Joan Williams was a devoted wife and mother. At 5'2 and3/4" she was small but she was a high energy go getter. Mitch always called her his "Energizer Bunny" because he could never seem to get her to slow down. From the moment she woke up till she went to bed she was all go and no slow. Besides raising five children she had started a very successful business teaching people how to cook, can, and garden. She was also a highly respected social media blogger whose commentaries and essays were carried on hundreds of

Today they rolled up the back roads towards Arlington each with their own squad by a separate route. Mitch was thinking of Joan and the boys while he prayed that America could be saved. He also spent quite a bit of time praying for his beloved wife and their two sons, "Lord help us each to do our duty and please God. Let my wife and boys come through this alive."

Ignoring the temptation to assault the captured Armory and PD station in Vienna the combined units of the Virginia Patriot Network maintained their focus to converge on the Virginia Hospital Center in Arlington.

Taking many different routes coming from all directions passing through small town after small town they picked up hundreds of police officers who were either members or sympathizers who took their patrol cars and joined the caravans. By the time the many streams of Patriots reached their designated staging area at Lacey Woods Park, five blocks from the hospital, complex they had been driving through ruin and devastation for many blocks. There were fires raging in houses and businesses. There where places where streets had been pulverized. Water mains were flooding wide areas, power lines were down, and bodies were strewn almost everywhere they looked.

"We can't stay here long," Mitch thought as he pulled into the fourteen acre park, "A few well-placed shells could take us all out."

Pulling his war surplus Humvee into the lot he could see that there were many more that had been bought at auction from the military. Many of the groups had at least one they had armored and armed themselves. The Dinwiddie Patriots had five of them. Using his ham radio Mitch broadcast, "I want all Group leaders to meet me at the park office."

Given the events of the day the park office was deserted, Mitch kicked in the door followed by the leaders of the arriving groups. Once they were crowded into the largest room they could find, a combination lunch/presentation room, Mitch said "All right we don't have long. The enemy may have spotters out here and a few rounds would devastate this park and everyone in it. Does everyone have a city map?" Knowing that city maps of all major cities in Virginia was a required part of the intelligence packet for every group he was glad to see every head shaking in the affirmative.

"We all know our Group numbers. I want all

Dr. Robert Owens

odd numbers to head east on Washington Boulevard then north on North Glebe Road. Peel off units on 15th, 16th, and 17th. The Unit that takes 17th should be big enough to split in two, with half working their way on side streets to the north side of the complex."

Just then there was a disturbance near the door of the room as two patriots hustled an Arlington PD Sergeant into the center of the room. Though he was obviously surrounded and outgunned the sergeant asked with all the authority he could muster, "Who are you people and what are you doing?"

"We are the Virginia Patriot Network, and we are here to kill those no-good bastards in the hospital," answered Mitch.

Without hesitation the sergeant said, "Thank God! I hoped you were really the good guys when I saw all the American flags. These invaders are wearing American military uniforms but they are flying ISIS flags," said the sergeant.

"Ya, we're the good guys and we are going to assault the hospital immediately," Mitch said to a chorus, "Kill the bastards!" "Let's go!" and chants of "U.S.A!"

"I see there many police vehicles from all over

122

the state here with you. Me and my command will join up too," the sergeant said.

Great!" said Mitch "Contact you precinct and tell them to send any tactical vehicles or equipment they have," he continued.

"Everything we had and most of our on duty staff were taken out by some high explosives and incendiary shells almost immediately. Our off duty personnel have been rallying to me and I have a force of about twenty men and six cars," said the sergeant.

"Fine, your force will join up with the even number assault teams. I want you right with me for your knowledge of the local area," responded Mitch.

Knowing this delay had taken precious minutes away from what needed to be a fast deployment, Mitch knew they had to disperse or risk coming under fire from the enemy's big guns. "I want the even numbered teams to head south on Washington Boulevard then north on North Greenbrier Street. Spread yourselves evenly along the perimeter sending enough units to join up with the odd numbered teams north of the complex."

Looking around the room he saw many faces that belonged to old friends and even the ones he didn't know personally he knew all of them had been training and planning for this day for years. They had tried using their votes, letters to the senators, representatives, and newspapers to wake the country up to the danger it faced from unrestricted and uncontrolled immigration and especially to the danger of bringing hundreds of thousands of un-vetted people in from the very stomping ground of the enemy all to no avail. Now that which they had long feared had come upon them. They were determined to do something about it.

"Fellow Patriots we all know many of us may not live to see the sun go down today, but by God we are not going to sit on our hands while the sun goes down on our United States of America!" The cheers and shouts were deafening. Mitch continued, "Let every man and woman do their duty. Let God guide our arms as we defend our nation, our families, and our way of life. And may God bless America!" Once again, the cheers and shouts were deafening.

"Let's roll!" Mitch finished off with the well-known network code words for full deployment and the leaders began leaving the room to return to their units and begin to implement the Patriot's plan to re-take the Virginia Hospital Center from the ISIS invaders.

As he walked out of the park office building he saw Joan, Jr., and Billy waiting for him. For a moment they all stood looking at each other knowing that by the end of the day some or all of them could be dead. Mitch embraced each of his sons. "Junior, Billy I'm proud of you. I always have been, but I've never been prouder than I am at this moment. You're Patriots and heroes." Turning to Joan tears filled Mitch's eyes as he embraced the love of his life. "My love, I hate these Islamic bastards for bringing this into your life. I'm so proud of you. You're not only the mother of this family, you're the representative of the mothers of this nation, and all I can say is if I had my life to live over I would have found you sooner so that I could love you longer."

Tears were also in Joan's eyes as she held the man she loved as she remembered the boy who had announced they would be married on the day they met. With her arms still wrapped around her husband she motioned with her fingers to her sons and soon all of them were mutually embraced in a group hug as she prayed, "God I commit my family into your hands. We are here fighting for the freedom of all, the freedom you have built into us as a necessary part of a godly life. We are fighting for Larry, and Bubba, and Sue. We are fighting for life, and I ask you to protect my family in this fight and give us the victory, in Jesus' name, amen.

Hating to leave the loving warmth of their family circle they reluctantly split off in separate directions, Joan, Junior, and Billy to the units they led and Mitch to the command unit. Soon the hundreds of vehicles packed into the park and standing in concentric rings for blocks in all directions began to disperse and follow Mitch's direction for their assault on the enemy.

Luckily for them, though the ISIS Strike Force did have spotters out in that area the spotters lost all but two members and their walkie-talkie was destroyed by a misplaced but very fortunate 9mm round from a now dead PD officer.

Consequently though their concentration had been spotted, it took a while for one of the spotters to make it back to the hospital and then to get to his commander. By the time high explosives began to rain down on the park from the 105 MM Abrams main guns there were only a few vehicles left that weren't on their way to deploy. The occupants of all those vehicles died. At about the same time the remaining spotter was located by a police patrol and eliminated so the enemy didn't know that the righteous indignation of thousands of American citizens was about to explode all over them.

CHAPTER SEVENTEEN

Fighting Fire with Fire

Truck 27 continued to pick its way through burning cars and around craters in the street heading to St. Elizabeth's. Since the attack by the snipers took out all of the tires on its right side the team from Firehouse 27 were forced to leave the squad vehicle behind. The members of the squad walked slowly, almost solemnly behind the truck since there was nowhere to ride.

Driving was slow because of the debris and because every moment they were expecting to have incoming rounds smashing through windows. Stop and go, stop and go they inched through the devastated residential neighborhood until Dogwood Street was completely blocked by a huge crater that was quickly filling from broken water mains. They hadn't encountered any more snipers since the skirmish at the metro station. Lisa and Lieutenant Edmonson continued to flank the truck on both sides moving as stealthily as possible from house to house.

Seeing there was no way to go any further and that they were still several blocks from their objective Lieutenant Edmonson keyed the microphone that hung on his left shoulder and said, "This is it. We aren't going to be able to make it to the hospital. Let's start with that house on the east side. Get some lines out. Start using the water in the truck. Jerry you take the rescue team and see if there is anyone needing help in there."

Immediately the well-trained firefighters jumped to action. Forgetting about possible snipers, ignoring the sounds of explosions and the smell of burning rubber, flesh, and tar shingles they efficiently began accomplishing their tasks. Knowing that with his best friend Lieutenant Williams dead the next in command of squad was Johnny Richardson, Edmonson said, "Johnny, take your men and figure out how we can pump water from the crater for a backup once the truck runs out."

Lisa was just about to leave her place of

concealment when Stage Four exploded into reality with the local impact of a supernova when one of the high explosive rounds made a direct hit on truck 27. Seconds later an incendiary shell landed at the far end of the same block and with a spray of napalm and magnesium a dozen houses suddenly changed from the cherished homes of families into their funeral biers.

The concussion knocked Lisa down and out. When she came to there was blood already drying in her ears, she had been cut on the wrist by glass shards, but she still had the AR-15 held tightly in her right hand. Shaking the cobwebs out of her mind Lisa sat up. Looking from her post between two houses and behind some thick bushes she could see a massive crater where moments before Truck 27 had stood. Knowing that with the truck gone there was no base for her team radio system she didn't waste any time trying to contact survivors. She crawled out from behind the bushes, stood up, and walked out to see the bodies and parts of bodies of her friends and co-workers spread all around the area.

Slowly others who could stand and walk emerged from the carnage. With no supplies there was little they could do for the many more who were wounded. Lisa slowly picked her way over to where Lieutenant Edmonson had positioned himself behind a gazebo. She found him right where he had fallen with a large piece of jagged glass protruding from the left side of his neck. He was obviously dead. She had known Edmonson since the academy, and he was the one who brought her to Station House 27 right after he was promoted and took command of the main truck at the house.

Looking at her fallen friend she thought of his four children and his wife who were now going to have to make their way without him. The anger rose in her until it was like a blinding light. Picking up his AR-15 and taking one last look at her friend, as the pool of his blood soaked the lawn beneath him, she turned back to the street. Enraged by the death of her friends and by the audacity of the invaders she wanted to see who was going to help her take some death and destruction in the other direction.

Walking up to the small band of firefighters who had survived first the sniper attack and now this total destruction of their ability to operate as a firefighting unit Lisa said, "Who's going with me to kill some of these terrorist bastards?'

For a moment no one said anything. Then Larry Johnson said, "Hell, I'm going home and take care of my family."

"Me too," said Abel Ozborn.

Several others shook their heads in agreement.

As if to justify his decision to go home Abel said, "There's nothing else we can do. All our equipment is toast and in all this," waving his hand to indicate the chaos around them...

"Who do we think is going to guard our houses and our families?" asked Betsey DeCost the newest candidate at the house.

Holding out the AR-15 she had taken off Edmonson's body Lisa said, "I get it. You all have families and I can't blame any of you for wanting to take care of them. But I'm going to the Hospital and see if there's anything I can do to kill every one of these monsters. Is there anyone who will go with me?"

Sharon Wells at 5' 5" and 130 pounds the smallest person on the team and the same one who had worked with Lisa to take out the sniper said, "Count me in."

Bruce Stattler, Bob Buford from Truck 27, and

Brian Bellingham, the sole survivor of squad all said, "Me too."

Handing the AR-15 to Bellingham, because she knew he was a retired SEAL, Lisa pointed towards the hospital and said, "Let's go fight some fire with fire."

They avoided the streets by jumping fences and circumnavigating pools, garages, and anything else that got in their way. They ran through backyards as they rushed to the sounds of the guns. A few hundred yards beyond the burning fire equipment they spotted two police cars that were sitting abandoned in the street. Stopping to look them over from a backyard they could see the windows and tires were shot out. They could also see one officer slumped over his steering wheel and the bodies of others lying in the street.

"Come on," said Billingham as he broke cover and sprinted to the cars. "Take the guns and any ammo you can find," he said as he reached in the nearest car and grabbed a shotgun. The others were hurriedly taking side arms and searching the bodies for back-ups. Moments later with several rifles they found in the trunks, two shotguns, at least one pistol each, spare magazines, and some extra ammo, the fire team was once again running through backyards on their way to their appointment with destiny.

They could now see the buildings of the hospital looming above the rooftops of nearby houses when suddenly they heard someone yell, "Hold it right there."

Instinctively they all dropped to the ground and with no direction or orders they had weapons pointing in all directions.

"This is Washington PD. You are completely surrounded and outgunned. Who are you and where are you going?"

"We're all that's left of the Firehouse 27 teams. All our equipment and most of our firefighters were taken out in an artillery barrage so we're on our way to kill some terrorists," Lisa called back.

"Lower your weapons and slowly get up."

"How do we know you aren't Islamist snipers?" asked Billingham.

"At least one of you step into the open so we know who we're dealing with," Lisa added.

Out from behind a large wheeled rubber garbage can that would have offered no actual cover from the AR-15s stepped a large man dressed in the uniform of a Washington PD Sergeant who held his hands up and said, "I'm Sergeant Bushings of the 25th precinct. We're gathering forces for an attack about two hundred yards from here. Will you join us?"

"If you're on your way to kill some of these no good terrorist scum we're with you," Billingham said as he got up without needing to consult with anyone on the fire team. They all stood up and soon they were joined by more than a dozen uniformed officers and a few civilians with a variety of hunting rifles and shotguns in the backyard that had once been the peaceful sanctuary of a hard working family.

"Come on we'll lead you to the gathering place," Bushings said. With no further consultation the combined group continued on through the backyards until they came to a larger open space that was formed by two backyards that had no fence to divide them. There they joined a group of more than seventy men and women, most in police uniforms, a few others in fire uniforms and more than two dozen civilians.

A man dressed in the uniform of a police lieutenant was standing on the back steps of the bigger of the two homes. He watched as the new group jumped the final fence into the gathering and then he asked, "Do any of you have combat experience?"

"I did three tours in the sand box and in Talibanistan and Billingham here is a retired SEAL," said Lisa.

"Great we're splitting up into ten man squads, and now we have enough combat vets to lead each team. The two teams that need a leader raise your hands. You two pick a team and every one, listen up." Once Lisa and Billingham had moved into their teams the police lieutenant continued, "They have the perimeter fortified and there are Bradleys interspersed with machine gun nests and riflemen dug in and sheltered behind cement road abutments. They have Abrams backed up into the building itself, there are snipers on the roofs. We've cleared out their snipers from the buildings around the perimeter, but there's no way to get to them except across open ground into concentrated fire."

The people in the staging area were quiet as they thought about what they were going to face. "Does anyone have any ideas how we can assault this place and not all die before we even get to the fence?" An awkward silence greeted the Lieutenant's question.

Finally Billingham spoke up and said, "We could get a few cars, start them up, tie off the steering wheels, block the gas pedals, and launch them at the perimeter from several locations and while they occupy the enemy we charge from another location."

"That's a plan," said the lieutenant "Does anyone have anything to add."

"We could set rag fuses in all the cars and maybe find the stuff in these houses or garages to make some Molotov cocktails to use in our assault," one of the other team leaders offered.

"All right let's get to it. You teams on the right side get the cars ready. You on the left get the Molotov cocktails ready."

Then someone said what all of them had at least thought of, "What about the patients and other hostages?"

"Obviously we need to try and avoid any collateral damage, but we can't leave them in there with these murdering terrorists. We have to try and do something," answered a man in civilian clothes holding a double barreled shotgun that used to belong to his father.

Either everyone agreed or at least no one made an objection. "Let's go. Every moment counts. Who knows when they might unleash another salvo that takes us all out before we get the chance to at least do something about this unprovoked invasion of our homeland?" said the Lieutenant.

With feverish activity the hodgepodge group of civil servants and civilians set about getting ready for an assault that would make the Charge of the Light Brigade look like a reasonable strategy.

CHAPTER EIGHTEEN

The Sword of Islam

As soon as the deafening roar of the Phase Four salvo had stopped reverberating off the walls of the Director's office in Walter Reed, Abdal El Shallub the first Governor of the ISIS Province of America said to his main communications officer Farouk Al Basaar, "Open all channels." Abdal knew there was no reason to shield their communications using game stations and low tech walkie-talkies any more. "And pipe the Caliph's coming announcement. Also tell our four radio stations to carry the announcements too."

"Yes sir," Farouk snapped as he then spoke into the headphone he was wearing which synched him up to all his communications officers. He was happy to follow his orders anxiously awaiting the great announcement. Abdal knew that since there was now push back at all locations in DC and in the four towns they had seized there was no longer any reason for any attempt at secrecy. Besides he also knew that there weren't many who would understand their open communications in Arabic. From now on it was just a matter of holding out and killing as many of the Unbelievers as possible.

As everyone in the room waited to hear from their leader reports began coming in about massive troop movements heading towards Water Reed and of smaller attacks around the perimeters of the other three hospitals. The fact that DC was a self-disarmed city had figured into the calculations of how long they could hold out and of how strong any civilian resistance would be. They knew that unlike the world they came from where every family had AK-47s and most had much more; America's capital had long been a gun-free zone.

"Command every Strike force to fire one hundred rounds from every Bradley into the surrounding neighborhoods and command Strike Force Four to fire two volleys from the Abrams they have facing east into Arlington

National Cemetery. That should enrage the Unbelievers enough to attack without caution into our guns."

"Yes, sir," Adnan Kaib his second-in-command responded immediately moving to make it so.

Just then the speakers overhead crackled into life as the long awaited announcement that had been planned all along to come after Stage Four raised the curtain on what they all believed would be the last act in their suicide mission.

On all four of the captured radio stations, on every radio station throughout their territories, and supposedly as news coverage on the radio and TV networks of Al Jazeera, in Arabic, Caliph Abu Bakr al-Baghdadi spoke to his devoted followers as well as to all Muslims within the sound of his voice: "Greetings Believers. Today is a day all of us have waited for our whole lives. This is a moment in History that generations of Believers have long dreamed of. Today May 10, 2016 I Abu Bakr al-Baghdadi, Caliph of the Land of the Believers by the Grace of Allah, announce that I am in possession of Zulfiqar, sword of Ali ibn Abi Talib given to him by Muhammad at the Battle of Uhud. This blessed weapon was found by my Warriors. Today I draw it from its sheath and declare unending Jihad against the Unbelievers until the last of the cursed boots have left the Land of the Believers, until the last of the Crusaders have been defeated and hides shivering with fear.

With this holy sword held high I call upon all Believers, Sunni and Shia, to set aside our differences and unite to defeat the Crusaders. We have more in common between us than we have differences separating us. The Unbelievers exploit our disunity to deprive us of victory, oppress our lands, kill our children, and dishonor our women. I call upon the Shia to leave your worship of the descendants of Ali ibn Abi Talib and the Ahl al-Bayt. Let us join together and usher in the blessed reign of the Mahdi.

I call upon all Believers in the Islamic State Province of America rise up. If you cannot strike against the government, kill your neighbors, attack anywhere you can, start fires, do anything you can to spread blood and fire in the den of the Great Satan.

Across the world we your Warriors are attacking their embassies, their military bases, and their industries. This day we shall let the hated Crusaders know their time is limited and that as the Sword of Islam is raised by a united faith soon our blessed black flag will fly forever over them and that their own children will one day shout with us, Allah Akbar! This holy sword shall not return to its sheath until victory is won and the Crusaders have bowed to Allah. There is no God but God and Muhammad is His Prophet, peace be upon him."

When the announcement ended everyone in the room shouted "Allah Akbar!" until they were horse.

"Farouk, loop that and play it as long as we have radio stations," Abdal ordered as he wiped tears from his eyes. "Let the Unbelievers know that they face a united people on a mission from God." Until they were knocked off the air every radio station throughout the ISIS territories and the radio and TV networks of Al Jazeera also kept replaying the announcement.

In the lead Humvee of the 13th Armored Brigade of the West Virginia National Guard Colonel Johnson wasn't listening to any radio broadcasts as he and his men unloaded their tanks and began planning their attack on Walter Reed Medical Center. The convoy had left I-270 in Bethesda, Maryland taking Old Georgetown Road down to Georgetown

Square. They moved through the large shopping area and began assembling the Brigade on the large open grounds of Walter Johnson High School. Colonel Johnson figured it was far enough away from Walter Reed to avoid any spotters or snipers the enemy may have deployed.

Setting up his headquarters in the gymnasium of the high school the Colonel soon had a communications hub and the command and control officers of his staff around him as the men outside readied for battle. In the midst of all the controlled chaos of military professionals setting up a command center Lt. Colonel Larson asked, "What about the hostages? How can we stage a full scale assault knowing they have thousands of hostages in there with them."

"Listen up everyone. We can't let consideration for hostages slow us down or make us ease up in our duty. We have to take back this facility. We have to clear these terrorists out of Washington, and we need to do it as quickly as possible. That'll be the most humane thing we can do for our hostages. Is everyone clear on that?"

"Yes sir" was the only answer heard from the assembled officers.

Johnson had been right that they were far enough out to avoid any spotters or snipers, but they weren't far enough out to avoid the Apache Shallub had ordered to fly cap.

As soon as the lone Apache reported there was American armor massing a few miles away Shallub ordered the other Apaches into the air to attack and to serve as airborne artillery spotters.

Only about three quarters of the Abrams were unloaded when the first hellfire missiles slammed into two semis carrying more tanks that were just entering the school grounds. The explosions were deafening. Immediately the already unloaded and manned Abrams using radar searched for the Apaches. Inside a dozen tanks gunners reported, "Target acquired."

"Fire," ordered commanders in every tank. The big 105 MM guns barked, the tanks rocked, and instantly there were three flashes as the enemy Apaches exploded. The one remaining ISIS chopper turned and headed back to Walter Reed followed by four National Guard Apaches. Before the commandeered chopper could get more than a few blocks it was a burning piece of wreckage falling from the skies.

At the same time shells from ISIS Abrams and from their self-propelled howitzers began to explode all around the school. Some of them landed in the football field, some hit the shopping mall, and some exploded in houses around the perimeter of the school. Watching the devastation out a huge window in the eastern wall of the gymnasium Colonel Johnson thought, "I'm sure glad those guys don't have GPS. Unfortunately they aren't so lucky."

"Bubba, have every piece of ordinance we have coordinate·with target tracking and return fire" Johnson said over his shoulder.

"Yes sir!" snapped Sergeant Hanks. Less than a moment after Hanks spoke the order into the headset hooked to his ear an almost mind numbing thunder announced that the order had been followed. Within seconds high explosive and incendiary rounds began landing with pinpoint precision all along the perimeter of Walter Reed. When the ISIS gunners fired back with their Abrams and self-propelled guns they learned what it meant to go toe-to-toe with a highly trained and battle hardened American Armored Brigade. It wasn't like fighting the Iraqi Army that melted away and left their weapons and vehicles as they ran. It wasn't like shelling the Peshmerga Kurdish Army that had all the will in the world to fight but lacked the weapons. No it wasn't like that at all.

While the rounds from the enemy weapons continued to fall ineffectively but with great devastation on the surrounding neighborhood the Americans used their extremely efficient and accurate return fire capabilities to zero in on the enemy positions and within moments of the enemy shells exploding there were American rounds landing on their positions. Two volleys were all the ISIS Warriors got off before their men were either dead or staggering around bewildered, wounded, or dying in the flaming wreckage of their once formidable arsenal.

The buildings of the Walter Reed complex shook and reverberated with the explosions of the incoming ordinance and from the secondary explosions from the targeted Abrams and Howitzers. The fire and smoke quickly made large portions of the complex unlivable death traps. Sprinklers and severed water lines did little to quench the flames driven by fuel and other chemicals used in the massive weapons.

The crackling yellows and oranges of the

flames and the billowing suffocation of the toxic smoke was a fitting addition to the hell that was playing out inside Walter Reed as it was in all four of the occupied hospitals.

It wasn't that the Warriors of the Caliphate were more inhumane in character than others. After the horrors of the twentieth century adhering to or following the Geneva Convention with its supposedly Marquis of Queensberry type gentlemanly war seemed quaint. In the twenty-first century the barbarism of past appeared destined to foreshadow the future. Even with this in mind the war crimes committed by the ISIS Warriors during their 2016 invasion seemed in retrospect to be over the top.

The key to understanding them was to understand one of the primary reasons for the invasion to begin with, theology.

Most non-Muslims know that the followers of Islam believe in and try to live by the Koran. Most do not know that just below the Koran in sanctity is the Hadith, or the collected oral sayings of the Prophet. It is in these sayings that are found the basis for Islamic Eschatology: the theology of the end times. This theology is believed by both Sunni and Shia although there are some minor differences.

Both believe that the end times will be ushered in by a great battle between two Islamic armies in the city of Deraa on the outskirts of Damascus. They believe this battle will culminate with the intervention of armies of unbelievers from the north and the west converging on Deraa. There in one cataclysmic battle the true followers of Muhammed believe they will be victorious and the glorious reign of the Mahdi, the prophesied redeemer of Islam who will rule before the Day of Judgment and will rid the world of evil.

With this in mind many of the atrocities they had perpetrated such as burning people alive, mass beheadings, beheading Americans, and destroying world heritage sites were done to provoke America into joining the Russians in Syria. Their goal was to draw the unbelievers from the north and the west to Deraa for the great battle. The Russians had taken the bait, but the Americans dedicated as they were to leading from behind had not.

From day one Caliph Abu Bakr al-Baghdadi had plotted and planned to bring war to America. When the unbelievable opportunity of the Obonyo Administration's open door policy was combined with the collapse of the southern border and with the millions of Islamic refugees from all over the world like a fifth column, ISIS was ready to strike. As massive and as destructive as the assault on Washington was the Caliph wanted to make sure it would provoke the response he was looking for. So he commanded his forces to not only rain the death and destruction of war upon America but to commit acts of brutality and senseless violence specifically chosen to infuriate and provoke.

In accordance with these orders barrages had been directed at Arlington National Cemetery and at such sacred places as the Lincoln Memorial, the Washington Monument, and the Smithsonian. And then there were the occupied areas, the four great Washington hospitals, and the areas within the four towns. Here they sought to humiliate America by systematically raping women, and killing innocents and noncombatants.

The women captives who had been rounded up in Rockville sat huddled on the floor of the massive gymnasium with the many women who had been rounded up in the hospital: candy stripers, volunteers, nurses, and doctors. They all sat huddled together while guards in fatigues with AR-15s walked around the walls or stood in small knots talking and smoking cigarettes.

The women were terrified. It had soon become obvious what was going on. Right after they had been herded into the room a few women tried to argue or resist. They were promptly shot in the head and their bodies lay scattered about the room bleeding. The rest of the women held their peace and cowered on the floor.

Then shortly after they had arrived the guards started grabbing women and dragging them out of the room. If they resisted too much they were killed. Since there was always at least two men grabbing each woman they couldn't struggle enough to get away no matter what they did. Some, especially the young and good looking, instead of being shot when they struggled were hit with a rifle butt from behind, knocked unconscious, and dragged out like a sack of potatoes.

It wasn't long before the first women came back from being dragged away. Some were naked clutching their clothing. Others were partially clothed. All were weeping and the word spread like news of the plague through the assembled women they were all being raped. The crying and moaning from the terrified women added to the horror as several groups of guards from every side of the room kept walking through the tightly packed crowd grabbing a woman here and another there.

In a small group near the center of the room sat Mary Harrington from Rockville. She didn't know for sure if her beloved Mike was dead but from the fact that these guards were wearing fatigues with patches for the 364th Armored Brigade from the Rockville Armory, where Mike was the night watchman certainly made her think that he probably was. No matter how that shattered her heart and no matter how much she knew that would be like the end of her life too she did not have any time to think about it.

Like the other women from Rockville she had been kidnapped from her home by some of these soldiers, forced onto a bus, and transported here. Once in the gymnasium she had located her best friend Sue Cummings, Jean her daughter-in-law, Ashley her daughter, and even Marsha Harrington her seven year old granddaughter.

Jean had a big bruise on the left side of her face, and Sue had a cut on her leg that Mary had bandaged with a strip torn from her nightgown. Like all of the women in the room these Rockville women tried to be as inconspicuous as possible keeping their faces on the floor and not daring to look up afraid that they would attract attention to themselves and be the next victim dragged out of the room.

The crashes from out-going and incoming fire, the shuddering of the building itself as rounds from the National Guard found their mark, the whiffs of smoke, and the sobbing and moaning of the women all contributed to make this as close as anyone would ever want to get to hell on earth.

The stories of what was going on were whispered from woman to woman without raising their heads or looking at who was speaking. Little Marsha was crying uncontrollably even though her mother, Jean, tried her best to muffle the sounds with her hands so as to not bring any attention to their little group.

As terrified as they were their fears rose beyond fever pitch when one of the groups of guards came over to their location and grabbed a woman right next to Mary. As they started to drag her away she yelled, "You'll have to kill me fir.." and a bullet smashed into the back of her head. They just dropped her body right there and then grabbed another young girl who was crying and shrieking, "Mom! Mom!" A woman next to her started to get up and was shot in the head collapsing into a pool of blood and brains spreading quickly across the floor. One of the men slapped the young girl, she couldn't have been more than twelve, so hard blood flew in several directions and she slumped in their arms as they dragged her away.

Most of the women who were brought back just laid weeping where they were dropped, but some managed to crawl back to their little groups. One such victim made her way to a group close enough to Mary's group for them to hear what she was saying. "They made me strip off all my clothes while they stood around me laughing and smoking cigarettes. A few of them burned me with their cigarettes. They handcuffed me hand and foot to a hospital bed, and then they raped me. I don't know how many. They just kept coming. I blacked out. Then when I was pulled out of the bed they told me to get dressed but I couldn't, so they dragged me back here naked. When they dropped me on the floor over there they dumped my clothes on top of me. Mostly they spoke to each other in Arabic, but many of them kept calling me whore and slut. I just want to die. I just want to die," the woman moaned.

Hearing this terrible tale made the Rockville women shudder and made Marsha cry even harder. A few moment later the woman who had been talking jumped up and started running and jumping over people towards the guards yelling, "I'll kill you bastar....." until a burst of fire killed her as well as several other women who were around her. The dead and dying from that incident lay in a tangled heap not thirty feet from Mary as she huddled on the floor praying.

About twenty minutes later, one of the groups of guards came and jerked little Marsha to her feet. Immediately her mother Jean leaped up to defend her and was shot in the face. Mary grabbed the leg of one of the guards screaming, "No! No!" until she was clubbed in the back of the head with a rifle butt. One of the guards hit Marsha in the stomach so hard with the butt of his rifle that she doubled up and vomited all over his shoes. They dragged her out. That was the last Mary ever saw of her granddaughter.

Such was the horror of what was later described as the ISIS rape rooms. Replicated in all four locations this war crime set the blood of every American ablaze just as it was designed to do.

CHAPTER NINETEEN

The Raptors Come Home to Roost

Coming to a hovering standoff about twenty miles from their objective, the Adventist Hospital, Colonel Stamper worked out the chain of command with the SEALS. All tactical units would retain their own commands. Therefore, Commander Nelson had been killed along with his entire command staff. It was agreed that Colonel Stamper would assume command of the entire attack force taking a Marine Major, Jim Delcans and a Navy First Lieutenant, Bob Nichols on as part of his staff.

Stamper requested and received the most up to date satellite pictures as well as everything the AWACS could provide. He shared all this electronically with each helicopter. On an encrypted channel he addressed the hundreds of men ready to follow him into battle, "Troops we are facing a well-entrenched enemy who has superior numbers and superior firepower. As we say in Delta Force and I'm sure you have something similar in the SEALS, the impossible may take a little longer but we'll get er done.

"Booyah!" came a loud response from many of the Navy and Marine copters.

"Here's the plan. Our only hope is to get low enough so that their positions are between us and those 105s. Each of our Delta Chinooks has a Bradley. What about the Super Stallions?"

"Ours are filled with Warhammers," responded Lieutenant Nichols.

"Great! We can use those Javelin missiles on the Abrams.

"We brought along a few M270 Multiple Launch Rocket Systems attached to our M993 carrier vehicles," added Major Delcans.

"All right men this is what we'll do. We'll maneuver in as low and as close as possible in the Chinooks and Sea Stallions. The Apaches and Cobras will stay far enough out so they can use maneuver and countermeasures on anything those 105s throw at them. At D hour the gunships will pop up and fire as many salvos into the perimeter as they can before the 105s start barking. Before the debris hits the ground the Chinooks and Sea Stallions will jump over the intervening houses and land us right at the door we just blew open. From then on we try to open as wide a breach as possible, kill as many terrorists as possible, and move in behind their perimeter. Our Intel shows that there're small groups attacking the perimeter from all directions, maybe they're police or just plain civilians with guns. Whoever they are hopefully they'll follow our lead and we can bring some numbers to bear."

"Any questions?" Stamper concluded.

"What about the Abrams?" someone asked.

"The enemy has backed them right into the buildings. I guess they figured that would stop us from trying to take them out so they have very limited to no maneuver capability. Once the dust settles the Apaches and Cobras should jump back up and empty everything they have on the Abrams."

"Any other questions?"

"Ya, what're we waiting for. Let's kill these assholes" one of the men said with his sentiment loudly echoed by many of the troops.

"All right let's roll," Colonel Rick Stamper said as his combined command of Delta Force and SEALS, the best America had to offer, braced for combat. These veterans of many engagements sat silently. Many were reflecting that after all those battles they were about to engage for the first time inside the United States and not in some far off outpost in one of America's far flung foreign operations. The gunships and the chinooks went low and took their positions like raptors on a wire as they prepared to swoop down upon their prey.

All around the Adventist Hospital scores of Americans, police, firemen, and many others armed with anything they could get were shooting from cover in the shells of what used to be solid middle-class homes. Hundreds were using the banks of Sligo Creek as a shooting position and kept up a continuous hail of bullets into the fortified perimeter of the hospital. Another hot spot was coming from Palmer Lane where people had built makeshift firing platforms inside the basements of destroyed homes. While all of these patriots were able to let the invaders know there was resistance to be reckoned with none of them could move forward in the face of the many Bradleys that lined the perimeter with their 25MM guns firing two hundred rounds per minute.

Most of this ragtag bunch was running out of ammunition and hope when without warning the entire corner of the perimeter at the junction of Sligo Creek Parkway and Carroll Avenue exploded in smoke and flame. Next there came the roar of the tanks and the howitzers sending their massive shells screaming overhead. As the dust settled from the explosions on the perimeter giant helicopters seemed to jump over the ruins on Palmer Lane and Jefferson Avenue to land in the green belt along the creek. Those who a moment ago were ready to retreat broke from cover and began running towards the gaping hole in the perimeter as they saw American troopers running out of the helicopters and into the fire from the hospital. As they all ran for the perimeter they were out paced by dozens of heavily armored Humvees. Some with 50 caliber machine guns mounted on top and all firing as they zoomed past.

Colonel Stamper had ignored the advice of his staff to stay in a rear position to direct the operation by saying, "The best place to direct a shock and awe engagement is at the tip of the spear." He was the first through the tangle of concrete and chain-link that a moment before had been the defensive perimeter of Strike Force Two. Stamper was closely followed by Lt Colonel Huffy Smith and the men of the combined Delta-SEAL team. The Special Ops teams were shooting right and left, yanking open doors of Bradleys and killing the dazed drivers. Jumping in they opened the rear doors and soon they had an American team manning the 25 MM gun and the machine guns. Instantly they turned their fire down the line widening the perimeter breach and spreading death and confusion among the ISIS Warriors unlucky enough to be in their vicinity.

On the heels of the team, the civilians began flowing in grabbing AR-15s from the fallen ISIS Warriors. They were soon providing a steady fire alongside the professionals as they beat the terrorists back in all directions.

In the board room of the Adventist Hospital Qasim Nassan the commander of Strike Force Two, was receiving a report from the runner for the commander of the perimeter, "Sir the Unbelievers have broken through on the southwest corner."

"Send reinforcements and beat them back."

"Yes, sir," the messenger said as he turned on his heels to run back to his commander. But instead he was knocked down as the whole building swayed and ceiling tiles fell.

Knowing that was not the sound or the feel when his heavy guns fired Qasim, holding on to a table to keep from going down asked, "What was that?" Then it happened again. By the time runners had alerted their commander of what was going on a third volley of Javelin missiles slammed into the building. Every Abrams on the south side and around the southwest corner had been taken out. The main building itself was on fire and secondary explosions marked the places where the tanks were now burning wrecks.

"We still outnumber the Unbelievers. Swamp them in numbers before they can get reinforcements" said Qasim as he regained his feet and his composure.

After the success of their initial surprise assault the combined team and their civilian reinforcements were holding their own, but they were no longer advancing as more and more guards from the perimeter left their positions and ran to join the fight. Soon more than a thousand were concentrating their fire as they brought up dozens of Bradleys to begin pouring led into the tangle of destroyed vehicles that provided all the cover the Americans had.

More and more ISIS Warriors rushed to the Southwest corner of the facility. Stamper on the front lines surrounded by his men was in the process of being overwhelmed. Rick dropped a magazine from his AR-15 and reached for another. He was out. He dropped the rifle and pulled his sidearm, a 1911 Springfield 45 that had belonged to his father and his father's father. He emptied a magazine dropping an Islamist with each shot.

As he was ramming another magazine home a terrorist jumped over the partial chassis of a dismembered Bradley he had been using as cover. He was knocked down by the weight of the man, his pistol flying out of his hand. He reached down and pulled out his 184 "Buckmaster" knife which had also been his father's. Deftly rolling the terrorist off his back and under him Rick plunged the blade into the side of his throat.

As he was getting up another Warrior jumped him from behind. He was about to stab Rick in the back of his neck when a shot from Huffy

Smith took him down. Rick regained his feet just in time for a bullet to ricochet off his helmet and send him down again as two more Warriors climbed over the ruined Bradley. His knife flew from his hand as he fell. As he crashed to the ground hard his right hand landed on a discarded AR-15. He pulled himself up and fired hitting both of the Warriors.

He could see all along the line that made up the furthest extent of their push into the hospital grounds. His troops were being overwhelmed by the masses of Warriors pushing in from up and down the perimeter. He could see no way to rescue the situation when suddenly he heard the roar of gunships overheard and explosions started impacting in the rear of the Warriors. The Warriors began to fall back in disarray as Rick and his team followed by the civilian patriots rushed forward yelling, "USA! USA!"

Behind Colonel Stamper and his force of Special Ops troops swarmed hundreds of enraged citizens who had seen what was going on from their hiding places in the rubble. They came armed with anything they could lay their hands on: shotguns, hunting rifles, pistols, axes, hatchets and some even with pitch forks and shovels.

Once they were on the hospital grounds they picked up discarded AR-15s as they stripped the bodies of the fallen Warriors taking knives, pistols, and hand grenades. They pushed forward following America's finest into the breach as they all slogged their way through the gaping opening made in the perimeter of the Adventist Hospital. Then following the gunships as they swept around the facility, they overran the terrorists. Within a few hours Colonel Rick Stamper, his Special Ops combined force, and the hundreds of civilians and police who had joined them were in possession of the entire perimeter.

CHAPTER TWENTY

Too Many Chiefs

In Arizona at Fort Huachuca President Parker was moving fast consolidating her power and dealing with the world-wide assault upon America.

She ordered General Zchevinsky, her newly appointed Chief of Staff of the Air Force, to launch the B-2 fleet for the Middle East with orders to flatten Raqqa, the de facto capital of ISIS. She ordered Admiral Davis her new Chief of Naval Operations, to command the Fifth and Sixth Fleets to launch every plane and every ordinance available at any known ISIS stronghold. She also ordered Admiral Davis to send every available marine and sailor with all available equipment to DC to take back the four hospitals with extreme prejudice.

She invoked Article Five of the NATO treaty and told every member government if there was not 100% response America was going to leave the alliance.

She called an emergency meeting of the Joint Houses of Congress to meet at Fort Huachuca immediately.

She nationalized all state police in Virginia and Maryland ordering them to take the enemy radios off the air and re-take the four captured police stations and airports. She also ordered any and all National Guard units that can be spared from the Battle of Washington should cooperate with the State Police and re-take those four towns ASAP once again using the term, with extreme prejudice.

Up and down the chains of command everyone was glad that someone was in charge. They all accepted her authority and appreciated the decisive manner in which she was moving to secure the capital, the homeland, and America's far flung outposts. They also approved her orders to launch massive attacks on ISIS.

Just as the newly reorganized power structure was beginning to get its feet on the ground marching to victory Mike Bender came into the big conference room that was the President's makeshift war room. The President was leaning over a long table filled with maps and Intel photos, "There're fire fights going on at all four hospitals. Do we know who these people are that are attacking the terrorists?" asked the President.

Interrupting before the assembled officers could answer Bender whispered in the President's ear, "Ma'am you're going to want to see this," as he handed her a folded piece of paper.

Looking exasperated at the interruption but knowing Mike would never interrupt her unless it was extremely important she opened the piece of paper and without changing her expression she read, "Speaker of the House Peter Bryan has just surfaced in northern Wisconsin where he was on a fishing trip and is calling a news conference in one half hour."

Pulling Bender off to a corner President Parker said, "Contact the head of the Secret Service and tell him to order Bryan's detail to bring him here immediately. No press conference and no communication with anyone. If anyone gives you any grief they can contact me directly."

"Yes, Ma'am," Bender said as he wheeled about and left the room to carry out his orders.

In just a few short hours the courageous and commanding way Parker had taken charge had rippled through the Federal hierarchy. The head of the Secret Service followed orders and much to his chagrin and despite his protests that, "I'm the rightful president," Representative Bryan was hustled onto a waiting plane and was on his way south within an hour of issuing his call for a press conference.

As the President returned to the conference table and as she listened to the reports and suggestions of her General Staff she thought, "I'm not going to let that progressive wimp with no military experience and no balls take over in the middle of this fight." And from Bender to the Director of the Secret Service to officers who hurriedly hustled the rightful president of the United States onto a plane, all thought just about the same thing.

Once again focusing on the Battle of Washington the President said to General Ed Brown the new Chief of Staff of the Army and the Chairman of the Joint Chiefs, "General I want gunships sent in to support the people attacking the hospitals. I want you to find out who is the highest ranking man leading these independent attacks, and I want you to promote him to a general officer and put him in command of the battle on the ground."

"Yes, Ma'am," General Brown said immediately turning to an aid to make it so.

CHAPTER TWENTY-ONE

The Family that Fights Together Prays Together

It took the Virginia Patriot groups almost half an hour to get in place. Once the even and odd number teams had joined up north of the complex they broadcast the agreed upon code word, "Touching."

Mitch took a deep breath and looked up and down the line of vehicles and patriots, police, and civilians, Americans ready to put it all on the line in defense of their homeland. Without any further hesitation he broadcast, "Let's roll."

Instantly the groups all took off towards the hospital firing everything they could as they dashed forward. The hodgepodge of weapons and lightly armored vehicles, as soon as they broke free of cover all along the perimeter, came under fire from the Bradleys. Firing 25MM rounds at 200 per minute soon the space between the smoking ruins of houses that gave them cover and the perimeter of the Virginia Hospital Center was littered with exploding and burning Humvees, jeeps, pickup trucks, and cars. The wounded were screaming as many of them became the dying and dead.

Every one of them had known that charging an entrenched enemy who had superior firepower and superior numbers was at best a risky maneuver and at worst a foolish one. And though many of the vehicles were hit others made the run unscathed and crashed into the infantry positions between the Bradleys while patriot snipers back in the ruined neighborhoods did their best to keep the enemy's heads down.

One of the first to make it into the grounds of the hospital was a privately armored Humvee that like many of the patriot vehicles had a big snow plow as an improvised bullet shield and battering ram on the front. He plowed through an infantry position running over several Warriors. Immediately the men inside and in the other vehicles that followed close behind him jumped out of their vehicles and engaged the enemy.

Ed Eastman, one of Mitch's oldest friends and an Air Force veteran with six kids and a large hardware business, was the first out of the Humvee. Ed was a big man, well over six feet and two hundred pounds of muscle and fanatical patriotic determination. Grapping the first ISIS Warrior he could get his hand on he placed the muzzle of his Glock 19 in his face and brought him down in an explosion of blood. Turning to his right he shot two more. Opening the door of a Bradley Ed shot the driver and as he pulled him out with his free hand he shot the man in the passenger seat before he could raise his AR-15.

All along the perimeter the same scene was playing out with many casualties as the patriots charged and encountered savage attacks once any of them made it to the defensive line of the terrorists. In just a few moments the patriots were turning the guns of captured Bradleys on the enemy occupied Bradleys that were firing on the charging patriot vehicles. Then they turned the 25MM guns on the warriors who were rushing up to reinforce the perimeter.

Mitch was out of the car shooting the fully auto

AR-15 he had modified himself into the packed ranks of the terrorists who were trying to regroup after being pushed back from the perimeter. While he was changing magazines he shouted over the din of battle into the microphone which was attached to the left shoulder of his fatigues, "Turn those Bradleys on the building around those Abrams. They have already weakened the buildings by backing the tanks into them. Do your best to make them collapse on the tanks and at least obscure their view. Watch out for those machine guns. Anyone with any kind of explosives try to disable the Abrams any way you can."

Taking magazines from dead warriors once his reserves were gone Mitch kept firing. He could hear the 50 caliber machine guns of the Abrams dealing death and destruction up and down the line. He wondered where Joan and the boys were, but he didn't have any time to do more than throw up a hurried prayer as he concentrated on leading his group toward the buildings.

Deep within the bowls of the Virginia Hospital Center the building resounded with loud noises coming from the assault outside. Though they knew an assault was going on the two Warriors

dragging an unconscious woman down a long
hallway from the main cafeteria where they
were holding the women hostages paid no
attention. One of the men had hit the woman
in the back of her head with the butt of his
pistol when she tried to resist them. They
were taking her to one of the rape rooms,
laughing and joking about what they would
soon be doing to the "Unbeliever whore," when
as they entered a junction of two major
hallways two men stepped up behind them and
using scalpels slit their throats. The Warrior on
the left died instantly dropping to the floor.
The man on the right was just a millisecond
behind his compatriot on the left but it was
long enough for the Warrior he engaged to
turn his head slightly to the left and that
stopped the assault from being instantly
deadly.

The Warrior dropped to his knees, grabbed his
throat with one hand while with the other he
letting go of the woman he grabbed his
sidearm.   Before he could get it fully out of his
holster the man on his back plunged the razor
sharp scalpel into the back of his neck instantly
killing him.

The two mysterious assailants stood up
breathing hard. At their feet were the two

dead Warriors in rapidly growing pools of blood. Between them was the unconscious woman. Following a plan they had worked out in advance they quickly pulled the two dead warriors into a nearby room taking their side arms as they did. Then they returned and dragged the woman back into the room. Returning to the hall using mops and buckets they had prepositioned against the walls they had hidden behind they cleaned up the blood and wiped up their bloody footprints behind them as they returned to the room and closed the door.

Quickly they used the mops to clean off their shoes. Then they went to the bodies of the warriors and stripped them of all their weapons and ammunition. After they had armed themselves they walked over to where they had left the woman. Using some smelling salts one of them produced from a front pocket they revived the woman. She woke with a start and immediately began struggling. She also yelled out, "No!" and then one man put a hand over her mouth as the other said to her, "We're Americans. You're safe."

The bruised, battered, and terrified woman looked from one man to the other. She could see they were not dressed in the fatigues of the invaders. Instead they were both dressed in the scrubs of doctors now partially obscured by the gun and ammo belts they had around their waists and slung Mexican bandit style from their shoulders.

"We're trying to find ways to attack these terrorists and we figured grabbing two that were busy with something else would be the best way to get some guns" said the taller of the two.

"Saving me was just a byproduct of trying to get some guns?"

"I guess it was," answered the other man.

"You can stay here. Maybe hide in that closet," said the first man as he pointed to a door at the back of the room, "While we go kill some more of these animals."

"I'm not hiding anywhere," said the woman as she got up "I served three tours in the sand box with the 32nd Infantry killing these guys and I want to kill a whole bunch more today. Give me one of those guns."

The second man unbuckled the belt around his waist that held a pistol and some extra magazines saying, "It sounds like you have more combat experience than either of us. My

name's Ed and this is Tom. We're both ER
doctors. We were both at lunch when all this
started. We were able to avoid capture and
have been sneaking around waiting for a
chance to get some guns."

"When we saw then dragging women down
that corridor we were able to find out what was
going on without getting caught. Then when
we saw that it was always only two men
bringing the women and that they were both
occupied dragging their victim that is when we
came up with our strategy" said, Tom.

"My name's Chelsea, I'm a rep for Phisher
Pharmaceuticals, and I was here waiting for an
early meeting with the head of the pharmacy
when these bastards scooped me up. Do you
know what's going on? Do you know what
they're doing to the women?"

"Yes we know?" answered Ed grimly.

"We've got to move," said Chelsea, "those
guys are going to figure out any minute that
their buddies are late with the next woman and
they will be looking for them. And the last
thing I want is to get captured again before I
get the chance to kill some of them."

"Come on we know where we can hide," said
Tom. Soon the three survivors were silently

moving down corridors from hallway to hallway in the huge building many people had often compared to a maze.

The two doctors seemed to know the twists and turns of the intersecting hallways like the back of their hands. Several times they had to hurriedly duck into closets and side rooms to avoid enemy patrols. They could hear the constant rattle of small arms fire interspersed with the deeper bang of the 25MMs on the Bradleys. Then as they turned down what Chelsea was sure was a hallway they had been down several times before they began hearing the roar of the 50 caliber machine guns.

After what seemed simultaneously like hours and just a few moments they were in a stairwell and then in a series of tunnels that ran in all directions making the maze of the hallways feel like an incredibly logical series of enameled straightaways. Five turns later and they were in a fairly large cement room that was filled with large air handling machines that were silently and efficiently running as if nothing out of the ordinary was going on.

As soon as they took up positions with their weapons aimed at the only door Chelsea said, "It sounds like the cavalry is on the way."

"What can we do now?" asked Ed.

"I say we try to recue those women in the cafeteria?" answered Chelsea.

"How many guards are there?" asked Tom.

"There must be at least twenty, but men are always coming and going taking women out, and bringing them back. My God it was so terrifying. They were killing women right in there if they resisted. It's a nightmare" said Chelsea as she shivered just thinking of the purgatory that was the cafeteria. Then she thought of the hell these two men had saved her from. "Thanks for saving me from those monsters."

"As much as I would like to save those women I don't think we can take on twenty guards" said Tom.

"Besides the best thing we can do for those women is to do something to help whoever it is that is assaulting this place. I don't know wha..." was as far as Ed got.

"Quiet! I hear something," Chelsea said as she grabbed Ed's arm.

In the silence that followed they could hear people walking down the corridor. They all gripped their weapons tightly as they crouched down and watched the door. When the knob started to turn they all prepared to fire. And all three breathed a collective sigh of relief when the door opened and a man dressed as an orderly stepped in followed by another dressed in the brown clothes of a janitor.

"Don't shoot we're Americans" the man dressed as an orderly said raising his hands as soon as he saw the two doctors and the woman in a ripped and blood stained dress.

"Come in and shut the door," said Tom.

He was surprised when the man in the janitor's clothes turned around and said over his shoulder, "Come on in we've found some more Americans with guns."

The first two men came in followed by more than a dozen others. Two were security guards who both had side arms. The rest were dressed in several of the distinctive colors and types of clothes that denoted the different categories of people working at the hospital There were a few nurses, a couple doctors, more janitors and orderlies, a candy striper, and even a couple of people in street clothes. Ed, Tom, and Chelsea were glad to see they also had a couple of AR-15s and regulation issue military side arms.

"I see you must have taken a few of the terrorists out too," Ed said.

"We did," answered one of the security guards, an older man with a deeply receding hairline.

"There are patrols down here," said one of the nurses.

"We've avoided all of them except one," said one of the doctors "And those guys wish we hadn't" he added as he held aloft an AR-15.

Being a natural leader Ed said, "All right folks what facts do we have?"

One of the nurses said, "These terrorists came in around daybreak. When they walked in to the main entrance people thought they were U.S. military until they shot the receptionist. I was in a hallway that opened up on the receptionist's desk. I saw all of that then I turned and ran."

One of the janitors added, "By the time they came down here I'd already heard lots of gunfire. I knew something was wrong, but everyone down here was fooled by the uniforms too. They swept our workshop with fire and killed everyone. Lucky for me when they came in I was in a storage room and I hid behind some barrels when they came in there to check."

"We all eventually met up one way or another down here. We were hiding out and moving from room to room avoiding several bands of terrorists that were moving from one area of the hospital to another. Finally we saw an opportunity to jump a group of three," said one of the orderlies.

The doctors knew Ed and Tom. One of them said, "Tom this gentleman here has a gun and he took out two of them and then Robert here and I were able to take the other one down."

"Bill and I were catching a few winks in the lounge when all this happened," filled in Steve the other doctor.

"Does anyone have military training or combat experience?" asked Chelsea. Several of the people in the group raised their hands. "Let's make sure these people have the guns" Chelsea continued.

One of the janitors spoke up, "I know where they have their headquarters."

"Where," several asked at once with everyone turning to the tall man with longish grey hair and a friendly face.

"I was able to see from the closet I was hiding in that they moved communications equipment into the Director's conference room before I saw the opportunity and made it down into the tunnels."

"Does anyone know what's going on outside?" asked Chelsea.

"Before I came down to these tunnels I was hiding in a room with a view right up 16th street and I watched as some kind of civilian, police mix with quite a few people in fatigues came up 16th and then rushed right into the perimeter which was manned by these killers. The Americans had some Humvees, jeeps, and pickup trucks. The terrorists had military looking vehicles with guns all along the edge of the property. The Americas just charged right into them. I could see it was happening all along the way from 17[th.] I could see up to 15th and everywhere people were rushing the guns. Lots of them died and some of the vehicles exploded, but they made it up to the hospital grounds, and that's what we're hearing. They're trying to fight their way in," said the Candy Striper.

Thinking of all the women she had left back at

the cafeteria Chelsea said, "We need to do whatever we can to help our people get in here."

"I could lead us through the tunnels. We could come out behind the murderers and attack them from the back," said one of the janitors.

The janitor who had seen the communications equipment arrive said, "Maybe we should try to take out their headquarters."

"Sure cut the head off the snake," said the man who had his own gun, a fortyish looking man who seemed to be paired up with a younger woman.

"How many grenades do we have?" asked Chelsea.

"I've got one."

"I've got two."

"I've got one."

Eventually they knew they had fifteen grenades.

"If we could get into that room we could take it out with less than half of what we have," Ed reflected.

"I can get us there if we can dodge or take

down any patrols we run into," responded the man who had suggested the plan.

"Let's do it."

"Ya, let's hit these creeps where they would never expect it then maybe we could make it down and still hit the other guys from behind," said, Tom

"Come on let's get these guys," said Chelsea.

Soon it was decided that they would head to the conference room for a grenade attack and then try to double back and hit the defenders from behind. It was an ambitious plan for less than two dozen people with less than a dozen weapons and a few hand grenades. But these Americans wanted to strike back. They wanted to attack these heartless monsters who had attacked them.

It wasn't unanimous though. They didn't speak up during the discussion, but when it came time to move out five people decided they would rather hideout and wait for it all to be over. The Candy Striper, one of the orderlies, one of the nurses, and to everyone's surprise the man with his own gun and his companion also said they were going to stay behind. When asked if he would let the people going on the attacks have his pistol he said,

"No way. I carry this thing to protect my wife and I and that's just what I'm going to use it for. I wish you all luck, but I'm no soldier and I'm no hero. My goal is for us to make it home alive."

With both groups wishing each other well they split up. The assault team moved out of the room and down the passage ways towards the conference room and the others staying there.

Once the bigger group was gone the man with the gun holding the hand of his companion also headed towards the door.   When the others started to follow him he turned and said, "Hey I don't plan on trying to hide from these killers with some kind of a crowd. You guys look out for yourself. We're going to go hunker down somewhere dark and out of the way." With that he turned back to the door and leading his lady behind him left the room.

The others decided to just stay where they were. "No one has found this room so far so maybe it will be all right. Let's hide behind these barrels and stuff and turn off the lights. They couldn't find a light switch so using a broom handle they broke out all the fluorescent light bulbs and crouched behind the barrels hoping to survive this nightmare.

CHAPTER TWENTY-TWO

The Charge of the Fire Brigade

They worked their way around from Dogwood Street through the Hebrew Cemetery which was pocked with craters from the many shells the terrorists could not resist wasting in desecration. Once again using backyards and all the cover they could find they moved up Congress Place SE to 15th. They followed Shippen Lane SE to Bruce Place SE until they made their way into the grounds of the Hayden Johnson Recreation Center. There under the cover of the canopy of the old growth trees they formed up their commandeered vehicles.

Along the way they surprised and eliminated two patrols. Then they came upon some abandoned police cars and several dead terrorists adding several more AR-15s, shotguns, pistols, some ammo, and dozens of hand grenades to their arsenal. They also picked up almost a hundred more volunteers who either came out of their houses or out of hiding and wanted to join in this valiant attempt to strike back at those who were profaning our sacred Homeland with their polluted mission of hate.

Knowing they had been lucky to have avoided drawing down any fire from the enemy's big guns, once they were in position they knew they couldn't wait long. Lisa, Billingham, and Sergeant Bushings, the three who had stepped up and whose leadership had gotten them this far, decided they would light up the vehicles they were going to send in as fiery battering rams and then come right in behind them just as they had planned.

"Let the battering rams hit and explode before moving to a full attack, and while the vehicle line is waiting for the explosions throw the Molotov cocktails" Lisa said sending her instructions up and down the line. "Everyone light your Molotov cocktails. Light the cars and let's roll!" Lisa yelled.

Those who couldn't hear her could tell by what those who could were doing that it was go time. Moments later forty cars took off careening towards the line of defenders at the edge of the hospital property. Close behind them came a line of Humvees, police cars, SUVs, pickup trucks and cars, with people shooting out of the front windows which had been removed and with others leaning out the side windows firing as well. Bringing up the rear was the force now numbering close to four hundred each with a Molotov cocktail ready to hurl.

Since all they had to cross was a single street there wasn't time for the Bradleys to have much effect on the onslaught of metal heading towards them at breakneck speed. The battering ram cars smashed into the enemy line with devastating effect. They plowed through the infantry and smashed against the Bradleys with a jarring impact. Then they burst into flames soon followed by an explosion. While the explosion was not generally enough to split open a Bradley its impact and concussion knocked the driver and the gun operators out of business long enough for the rest of the assault plan to unfold.

Holding back until the battering rams exploded the leading vehicles of the attackers took quite a bit of fire from the defenders. Then the attacking patriots got up close behind their companions in the vehicles and they hurled the Molotov cocktails into the midst of the massed defending infantry. Soon the screams of burning men mixed with the smell of burning diesel and flesh created a nightmarish scene fit for the lowest circles of Dante's inferno.

Then the Patriots drove their vehicles into the burning and confused defenders running them down and quickly jumping out grabbing up fallen rifles and smashing their way into the Bradleys. Soon there were numerous Bradleys taken over by Americans swiveling their turrets and firing into the streams of enemy infantry that were already coming to plug the gap.

Lisa stood side-by-side with Sergeant Bushings each firing magazine after magazine into the onrushing Warriors who kept running into the muzzles of their guns from what seemed like a never ending supply. They didn't know it but General Malouf had commanded the leader of Strike Force Three, Abdahl Baroun, to do anything he could to break the assault. Consequently since he saw no other assault he was emptying his perimeter and sending everyone against Lisa and her team.

Two things happened simultaneously just as Lisa and the team were beginning to break through towards the buildings. One, the 50 caliber machine guns on the Abrams opposite of Lisa's position opened up. And two, seeing the enemy abandon their positions along the perimeter other patriots singly and in small groups started rushing the hospital. Soon there were pitched battles going on all along the perimeter with many Americans breaking through. In the confusion of close quarters fighting the bullets from the ISIS Abrams' 50s were hitting as many of their own men as they were hitting Americans.

Even with the losses being heavy on both sides the fire from the 50s stopped the forward momentum of the Americans. They sought whatever cover they could find and began trying their best just to hold on. The 25 MM rounds from the Bradleys were bouncing off the Abrams.

"We're going to have to withdraw. There's no way we can rush into those 50s," said Brian Billingham.

Lying between Billingham and Lisa while still firing under the Bradley that was giving them protection Sargent Bushings added, "The Fireman's right. We have to fall back."

Looking at the battle scene she could see that the Americans were now pinned down and that more reinforcements were arriving constantly as terrorists from all around the perimeter rushed to give their compatriots assistance. "We'll get wiped out if we try to run back to cover," Lisa said as she looked back and tried to imagine what it would be like running with their backs to the enemy across that open street.

"I know, but I don't see any alternative. If we stay here all of us are going to die. If we withdraw some might make it," said Billingham knowing that most would not.

"All right I guess it's our only choice." Lisa was just about to start yelling "Withdraw!" when huge explosions wracked the building in multiple places at once. The 50s fell silent. Smoke was pouring from the building wherever the Abrams had been pulled into them. The noise, the concussion, and the billows of black oily smoke were but a prelude to numerous secondary explosions that were still ringing in their ears as the Patriots heard Lisa yell, "Attack!" or if they couldn't hear they saw her. Billingham and Bushings jumped up and started running into the faces of the shell-shocked and bewildered terrorists.

They had no idea who had silenced the Abrams and their deadly 50s, but they instinctively knew what to do about it, "Attack!"

All around the buildings of St. Elizabeth's Hospital the Abrams were now burning hulks. The thin line of self-appointed minutemen and women were clutching weapons that moments before had been trained at them as they rushed to take back American ground. With the Patriots turning the Bradleys around to fire at the terrorists, while shooting, and throwing grenades many of these dedicated suicide Warriors got their wish and died a martyr's death.

Inside the hospital teams of Warriors were putting the finishing touches on booby-traps and bombs. They always knew this was a suicide mission and in their hatred of all but themselves they were determined to take as many Americans with them as they could.

There were guns to the right of them, guns to the left of them, guns in front of them that volleyed and thundered. They were stormed at with shot and shell. Boldly they ran, into the jaws of Death, into the mouth of hell. Someone blundered. Someone left the gates unguarded and the watch was asleep. Someone allowed these wolves of hate into our once inviolable land. Those who fought had not done it. Their reckless and naïve leaders had. But in their sturdy and courageous response to this cold blooded attack they did not take the time to blame those responsible. They did not reason why. They just accepted the burden of the common man in the wars brought upon them and they realized theirs was but to do or die.

CHAPTER TWENTY-THREE

Death From Above Fire From Below

The conference room that the ISIS Governor of America Malouf Shallab had chosen for his headquarters buzzed with activity. There were many Warriors monitoring communications. On the many screens which carried all the closed circuit TV surveillance both inside and outside Walter Reed which the ISIS techs had re-routed from the security office to the conference room. There were several Warriors manning communications gear constantly linked to the companies on the perimeter, both giving orders and receiving reports. They were also in constant touch with the many spotters and snipers on the roofs of the hospital and throughout the neighborhoods around the complex.

Bassam Kassab the Commander of Strike Force One reported to the Governor, "Excellency we have fired for effect on the American positions. The spotters who remain are reporting the results so that our gunners can adjust their fire and take out the Unbeliever's armor and...." Then the building felt like it lifted up and then fell right back down as the deadly accurate American counter fire took out the ISIS Abrams. Ceiling tiles came down in an avalanche; the lights flickered and then stabilized. Dust and smoke filled the air. Some of the communications gear blew up from the power surge others stopped working as circuits tripped, reset, and then tripped again.

Bassam had been thrown down hard hitting his head against the metal leg of a table knocking him senseless. The Governor was also knocked down but not out. His left cheek was bleeding and his ears were still ringing from the concussion when he struggled to his feet and called out, "Find out what happened!"

The people in the headquarters were still picking themselves up when the first runner came in and reported, "Excellency the Unbelievers have taken out the Abrams and they have landed a heavy barrage all along the

America's Trojan War

perimeter."

"Get to the roof and bring me a report. Tell the spotters to establish radio contact with headquarters immediately then you come back and give me a report."

The communications were now coming back on line. Commander Bassam was once again on his feet blood streaming down his face from the big cut on his head. He used his black headscarf to tie around his head which slowed but did not stop the flow of blood. He went over to the reviving communications area calling back to the Governor, "There are fires in many areas and parts of the building have collapsed."

"Ah the Americans were not restrained by the hostages. Perhaps now that their Denier-in-Chief is gone and there is no one to apologize for their power America has found a leader who will fight," said the Governor.

One of the radio techs called out, "We are now in touch with spotters on the roof again and they say they can see American armor rolling down Old Georgetown Road."

Confused moment followed confused moment that ticked by in the dusty room filled with dedicated and determined Warriors then a

199

communications tech called out, "They have turned east on West Cedar Lane."

Runners came and went. Orders and exhortations to stand firm were sent by Basham Kassab to his many different units. Then another communications tech called out, "One company is continuing east on Cedar Lane. Three companies are heading south on Rockville Pike."

Soon the same tech called out, "The company on Cedar Lane is spreading out in attack formation."

"Are all the charges and booby-traps set?" asked the Governor.

Yes, Excellency. We will bring the hulk of this building down upon the Unbelievers. It will become their tombstone" responded Kassab.

"Order the patrols to go through the rooms and kill every patient. Tell the guards to quit educating the Unbeliever whores about what it means to be unsanctified, uncovered, and unholy. Have the guards kill all the women except for fifty who have been educated. Take them out and release them through the perimeter so that the Americans will know what we've done to their women."

"Yes, Excellency," Kassab said. He then turned to an aid and told them to relay the Governor's orders to the corridor patrols, the hostage guards, and the men in the rape rooms.

Just then a communications tech called out, "The Americans have two companies on Rockville Pike and they are posted in attack formation. The final company is heading east on Jones Bridge Road."

"Rejoice my brothers the moment of our glorious martyrdom grows near. It will be our honor to present our beloved Caliph with such a funeral pyre burning into the black soul of the Great Satan that our ultimate death and defeat will blossom into the greatest victory in the History of all the Believers who have ever lived. And though we die we have claimed this, the Province of America for the Glory of Allah and the honor of his prophet Muhammed, peace be upon him" said the Governor.

Cries of "Allah Akbar!! Allah Akbar!!!" filled the room

Looking to his leader Bassam Kassab said, "The Americans are going to surround us before they attack," as he used a handkerchief someone gave him to wipe the blood that was running freely under the blood soaked makeshift bandage he had tied around his head.

"Tell the Bradleys to hold their fire. Don't waste anything on the Abrams and aim at the infantry, the trucks, and any Strikers they see" called the Governor to his communications center.

One of the techs answered back, "Excellency our spotters are reporting that the Americans have stopped where Palmer Road meets Jones Bridge Road and that they are getting into attack formation."

For the first time since the building had bucked and it was obvious that the Americans were no longer going to act as the Caliph liked to say, "Like foolish boys too mad to run and too afraid to fight," Bassam Kassab smiled as he turned from the communication techs and said, "The fools are leaving the east door open," to Abdal El Shallab, first Governor of the ISIS Province of America.

Immediately seeing what he perceived as a golden opportunity to increase the Americans' casualties Shallab, the veteran of hundreds of battles, the man who had personally ordered the beheading of four Americans in Raqqa in front of the Caliph himself said, "Have all the infantry from the entire perimeter move to the east side of the building. They will do nothing to stop the Abrams and the Bradleys will be able to chew up their infantry as they advance just as well without infantry support. Once they are on the east side as soon as the Americans begin to advance order our infantry to divide in the middle with one group going north and the other south. They should circle around the east ends of the Americans and fall on their infantry from behind."

"Yes Excellency," Kassab said turning to an aid to transmit the orders by runner as well as by radio to make sure everyone knew the plan. "This will give us a chance to send more of these devils to Hell before we make our journey to Paradise" Kassab added again smiling even though the loss of blood was beginning to have an impact on him.

As a dull roar grew into a pulsating ear pounding deafening hurricane of sound, a communications tech shouted to make his voice heard above the din, "Excellency the spotters report that there are many Apache gunships coming from all directions."

"Ah the Americans must have found a military leader to equal their great General Schwarzkopf. This will be no fight against soldiers not allowed to fight. Today we will meet the Americans warrior to warrior and as we take their lives we will gain even greater glory because we are killing brave men even if they fight for the Great Satan. These are not the handcuffed boys their former leaders sent as sacrifices upon the altar of death for their vain attempts to steal our lands. Today we will see."

As deafening roars added to the ear shattering noise of the massed Apaches a communications tech called out, "Excellency the American Apaches have obliterated our perimeter. There are exploding Bradleys everywhere," interrupting the Governor's speech.

"Just what I would have done," said Bassam Kassab the commander of Strike Force One.

"As would I, as would I" replied the Governor. "The assault will come on the heels of that barrage. Tell the infantry to prepare to move out to the east."

"Excellency there is no infantry left. The perimeter is aflame everywhere. Your order was too late, no one could have moved before they were caught in the rain of fire" said one of the communications techs.

Kassab, standing near the tech who had just spoken up, stepped up behind him, drew his pistol and shot the man in the back of his head. "His excellency didn't ask for advice or commentary. He gave a command. Transmit the order."

With no hesitation all of the techs transmitted the order for the now nonexistent infantry to prepare to strike out to the east to envelop the Americans.

"Bassam we shall soon be together in Paradise with all of our old comrades feasting with Saladin himself and all the other Believers who have gone before us fighting the Crusaders and dying in......" Suddenly the room dissolved into twisted wreckage, bleeding bodies, and flashing sputtering equipment as the ceiling preceded the roof in a race for the floor. The whole building seemed to raise itself up and then quickly fall in on itself. The incoming Hellfire missiles took out supporting walls, and in some areas three and four floors all collapsed into a smoking pile of rubble.

Having destroyed the enemy armor and shattered their perimeter Colonel Johnson led the 13th Armored Brigade of the West Virginia National Guard south down Old Georgetown Road. They turned east on West Cedar Lane to attack across the campus of the Stone Ridge School of the Sacred Heart. Colonel Johnson sent one company of the Brigade east on Cedar Lane.

With the other three companies he proceeded south on Rockville Pike. He left two brigades on Rockville Pike and sent the final company east on Jones Bridge Road. Having surrounded the hospital on three sides with his armor he was just about to order the attack when the radio in the back of his Humvee came to life, "Come in West Virginia 13th Armored this is the 337th Combat Aviation Brigade out of Bolling Air Force."

Surprised and shocked Colonel Johnson told Master Sargent Randall Hubbs his comm tech, "Hand me that microphone Hubbs."

"Yes sir," Hubbs replied as he handed the radio's microphone up to the Colonel.

"Come in 337th Combat Aviation Brigade this is Colonel David Johnson commander of the 13th Armored."

"Good morning Colonel this is Colonel John Greenstein commander of the 337th Combat Aviation Brigade. I have some good news for you. We've been ordered by the President to give you all the air support you need."

"Wow! I'm glad to hear the President survived the attack. We had heard he was dead," Johnson said. He had never been a supporter of the president and he blamed him personally for the very situation he was in but he was glad that the man in the office had survived.

"I'm not talking about President Obonyo. He was caught in the first barrage along with just about everyone else in his chain of command. I'm talking about the new President, Patricia Parker" responded Colonel Greenstein.

"President Parker? I never heard of her. How did she become president?"

"Don't know and don't care Colonel. I guess she was a cabinet secretary or something. Any way she has been sworn in and my Commanding General says she is the president. Myself, I just salute and take orders. I'm just glad someone has taken command who isn't afraid to act like America is the most powerful country in the world. Somebody told me she is a retired officer with combat training, and as far as I can tell she's acting like it."

Without taking even a moment to reflect on the momentous news Johnson did the verbal equivalent of saluting and taking orders when he said, "That sounds good to me. Here's the situation Colonel. My 105s took out all the Abrams and we have punctured the perimeter on all sides. I was just about to order a full assault on three sides. Instead if you could pulverize the perimeter then give us cover when we roll while sealing the east side we should be able to smash our way into these buildings and mop up these ISIS terrorists in short order."

"Roger that. Hold back until we light up the perimeter then let it roll."

"All right Colonel Greenstein let's give these intruders a taste of good old fashioned American death from above and fire from below."

With that the 13th stood its ground ready to advance. A short time later the roar of massed Apaches pounded against their ears with the intensity of a base drum in a small empty room. Suddenly the sky was filled with gunships firing hellfire missiles at points all along the perimeter. Fire and explosions ripped the day open as shattered bodies and vehicles flew in all directions.

"Colonel Johnson how about a barrage into the building before we take up our positions as

your air cover and close the eastern door?"
asked Colonel Greenstein.

"Those buildings are filled with thousands of
hostages," Colonel Johnson answered.

"The President has ordered that we should
assault the enemy with extreme prejudice and
worry about the hostages after the facilities
have been retaken."

"I guess we do finally have a fighting
President. Sure bring the roof down on their
damn heads and let those sons-a-bitches know
they're messing with the U.S. armed forces
without our hands tied behind our back for
once."

Almost instantly every Apache launched one
Hellfire directly into the building. The
explosions were followed in some areas by the
collapse of roofs, in others by jets of fire
exploding out windows, and in yet others by
huge columns of smoke that leapt into the air.

Just moments later, the Apaches had taken up
positions, sealing the eastern side of the
complex and some hovering over the armored
columns. Looking at the crumbling and
burning building surrounded by a blazing
perimeter Colonel Johnson commanded his
men into battle. He had done this many times

before in Iraq and Afghanistan but this was the first time he or any other commander ordered an assault by an American military unit in the United States since the Civil War.

Being from West Virginia where the Civil War seemed like it was just last week the significance of this did not escape the Colonel. Looking straight ahead and speaking to no one in particular he said, "Nothing will ever be the same."

Behind him Lieutenant Colonel Bobby Larson thought about his little four year old son, "Junior, you'll never even get to know the America your Dad grew up in," then he said, "War always changes things, but I have a feeling this war is going to change everything. We aren't just attacking a hospital we're going through the looking glass."

Sargent Bubba Hanks driving the Humvee added, "Maybe it'll be better. At least now we have a president who'll let us fight. Maybe this time we'll be allowed to win."

"We may win Bubba but we need to remember what we're fighting for not just hate what we're fighting against," Colonel Johnson mused. Then all conversation ceased as they and the rest of the 13th made contact with the enemy.

CHAPTER TWENTY-FOUR

Four Assaults Become One Battle

Inside a captured M1126 Stryker Combat Vehicle Colonel Stamper was holding a meeting with his commanders. There was Lieutenant Colonel Huffy Smith, Stamper's second-in-command; his company commanders Captain Jim Grady, Company A; Captain Joe Kearnz, Company B; and Captain Mahmoud Sarraf, Company C. They were joined by Marine Major, Jim Delcans and a Navy First Lieutenant, Bob Nichols of the SEALS as well as Major Jim Helverson the commander of the Apache Attack Wing.

The officers were in the back of the Stryker discussing how to proceed now that they had the perimeter under their control. There was still sniper fire and some very concentrated fire coming from the buildings. However once the terrorists started firing and their location was pinpointed by their own muzzle flashes, fire from the Americans soon convinced them to switch location. There didn't seem to be any coordination to the attacks.

As the officers weighed first one course of action then another First Sargent Julie Barns, Stamper's communication tech, called through the vehicle intercom, "Colonel Stamper I've just received an urgent message from Major Jenkins back at Fort Hamilton."

"What is it?"

"He said that by order of the President you have been promoted to Brigadier General and you are to assume command of the assaults currently underway at all four hospitals in DC."

"I thought the President was dead?"

"I asked Master Sargent Welling about that Sir and she said there's a new president that was sworn in out in Arizona. She was the most senior surviving Cabinet Secretary. She's a retired Colonel named Patricia Parker."

"I know Patty Parker," said Major Jim Helverson. "I served under her in the sand box. She's one damn fine officer. I never knew a woman or a man who was more kick ass and take names when it comes to facing the enemy. If she's the new president we're going to see a 180 degree turn and these ISIS assholes have some hard times on the way."

Accepting the promotion and his new responsibility as he always accepted any order Stamper immediately began transitioning from what he had been doing to what he was now ordered to do, "Is there any communication available to the other locations."

"I'll ask," said Sargent Barns. In a moment she added, "Yes sir Fort Hamilton has been able to contact the Colonel commanding the assault on Walter Reed, but no one has been able to raise the assault forces at the Virginia Hospital Center or at St Elizabeth."

Everyone in the Stryker knew Stamper needed a few minutes to think so they waited patiently even as small arms fire continued to ricochet off the vehicle and the sounds of the on-going battle reverberated in the metal shell.

A gifted strategist as well as a tactical thinker with years of command experience it didn't take Rick long to decide what to do. "Huffy I'm appointing you to command Delta Force and the combined operation here. Major Halverson

I need you and half your Apaches to come with me as I set up a unified command. Appoint your second-in-command to use the five remaining Apaches to provide ground support here under the overall command of Lieutenant Colonel Smith."

Rising, Rick continued, "Come on Halverson we have a four pronged offensive to coordinate. Men I'm leaving this battle in your capable hands. Get in there and kill these bastards."

"Yes sir!" they all said at once as Rick and Major Halverson stood and left the Stryker.

As soon as the two officers were gone the remaining six went back to their plans for an assault on the buildings. They were soon joined by Captain Ron Rogers the man left behind to command the Apaches.

The officers decided that the best way to proceed was straight ahead. Assault the buildings now before the enemy has time to regroup. Huffy turned to Captain Rogers and said, "Rogers I want you to stand off with the Apaches. Keep the roofs free of spotters and snipers. If we need you to target something we'll let you know."

"Yes, sir," Rogers answered.

As they were leaving the vehicle to return to their commands Huffy added, "Keep your ears on. We need to keep each other aware of where everyone else is to avoid any friendly fire incidents and to make it easier to concentrate our forces if, when, and where we need them. Give me Delta sign when you're ready for the assault."

It took about twenty minutes for everyone to get in place. Soon the radio announced "Delta Alpha," "Delta Charlie" than after a moment's delay pregnant with anticipation, "Delta Bravo."

"Let's roll," Lieutenant Colonel Bill "Huffy" Smith called into the radio as he began what he knew would be the decisive command of his life; the final assault on the Adventist Hospital in Washington, D.C.

Inside the hospital Mahamoud Abzaak the Commander of Strike Force Two was speaking to his second-in-command Hussain El Komar, "Are the charges and booby-traps all set?"

"Yes sir!"

"Round up about fifty of the Unbeliever whores who have been educated and run them into the enemy lines. Kill the rest of them. Send your men and have them kill all the patients."

"Yes sir!" Hussain answered turning immediately to the communications tech to make sure the orders went out.

"Well Hussain, today will be a glorious day to offer our lives for the service of the Caliph and the glory of God."

"Yes, Mahamoud it seems like just yesterday we were boys in Khan al-Shih dreaming of a day when we could join the holy martyrs and strike a blow against the Great Satan."

"I know my brother. Our families will be so proud when they hear of the great victory we have been privileged to be a part of right here in the heart of darkness."

Speaking now to the whole room Mahamoud Abzaak the Commander of Strike Force Two raised his voice and said, "My brothers. Allah has chosen us to join his Holy Martyrs. This day we will join the brothers who have gone before us and this day we will feast in Paradise."

Shouts of "Allah Akbar!! Allah Akbar!!!" filled the room as Mahamoud continued, "Today we have driven a stake into the heart of the Great Satan. We have shown them that they are safe nowhere that even here in their Crusader capital we can kill their people, desecrate their dead and ravage their women. Soon they will grovel in total defeat before the feet of our Caliph as the Sword of Islam severs the head of all Unbelievers and heretics at the coming Grand Battle of Deraa. Today no one dies in vain. All die in glory!"

Once again, shouts of "Allah Akbar!! Allah Akbar!!!" filled the room.

Kicking in doors, jumping through windows, dashing through holes in the walls from explosions the combined Delta Team-SEAL force followed by hundreds of enraged police and armed citizens stormed into the buildings that comprised the Adventist Hospital.

The Warriors inside were battle hardened in hundreds of engagements, determined to make the Americans fight for every room and every foot of hallway, and they were dedicated to dying as martyrs for their Caliph and for their God. It was slow going. Grenades were flying in both directions and the sound of small arms fire was constant. Several times when they were blocked the Special Ops team called in strikes from the Apaches which cleared rooms and shattered resistance until they got to the next intersecting corridor. Inch-by-inch step-by-step the Americans pushed the invaders back until they had cleared the first floor and then they began fighting their way up the stairwells.

Having moved the five Apaches and the Chinooks he had taken for his Mobile Command Center a few blocks from the Hospital, Colonel Stamper was connected to Colonel Johnson of the West Virginia National Guard who was regrouping after his men had taken control of the perimeter at the Walter Reed Military Medical Center.

"Colonel Johnson this is General Stamper I've been appointed by the President to take over all command of the assaults on the captured hospitals."

"Looks like this new president means business," Johnson answered

Expecting to be questioned about the president Stamper asked, "How do you know about the new president?"

"The 337th Combat Aviation Brigade out of Bolling Air Force showed up and paved the way for our assault on Walter Reed. Their commander told me about the new president."

Glad that he wouldn't have to go into any explanations to get his authority accepted Stamper asked, "What's your situation?"

"We've taken the whole perimeter, taken out their Abrams, and knocked their Apaches out of the air. Right now I'm waiting on the arrival of the 24th and the 11th Brigades of the West Virginia National Guard for reinforcements before we storm the buildings."

"Colonel I don't know if you've been advised but the West Virginia National Guard has been nationalized by the President."

"Yes Sir, General Corbaine shared that Intel with me a little while ago."

"Is that Crash Corbaine you're talking about?"

"Yes sir it is."

"I lost track of Crash after he retired. I didn't realize he was even from West Virginia. Anyway I see you have the situation well in hand. Listen I don't care who is the senior officer out of the three brigade commanders who'll be active at Walter Reed. You're the first man on the scene and I'm appointing you to take command of all three brigades and clean those terrorists out of there."

Knowing he wasn't the senior officer out of the three he accepted the assignment but asked, "If I have any push back from the other brigade commanders can I have them contact you sir."

"Yes of course Johnson. You take command and if anyone has any questions you have them contact me.

When he was done speaking with Colonel Johnson Stamper told his communications tech to try every frequency possible to see if he could raise anyone at either The Virginia Hospital Center or St. Elizabeth's.

Moments later the tech said, "Colonel I have a man on the horn using ham radio who says he is in command of something called the Virginia Patriots who are assaulting the Virginia Medical Center."

"Put him through sergeant," Stamper said.

"This is General Stamper of the United States Army who am I speaking with?"

"This is Mitch Williams and I'm the leader of the Virginia Patriot Network."

"Mr. Williams how many troops do you have?"

"We arrived with a little over two thousand and we picked up volunteers and police along the way. I would say we have probably three thousand now. All are armed and ready for the fight."

"Mr. Williams are you a vet?"

"Yes sir, I retired after twenty years."

"What was your rank when you retired?"

"I retired as a captain sir."

Not knowing whether or not he had the authority to do so Stamper said, "Captain I'm re-activating you as of this moment. I'm giving you a field promotion to Colonel and appointing you as the overall commander of the assault on the Virginia Hospital Center. I'll dispatch some Apaches to give you air support and anything else I can send. If anyone gives you any guff tell them to contact me."

"Yes sir!" answered Mitch. As soon as the radio went silent he returned to the business of leading the assault on the hospital buildings.

"Sargent, have you reached anyone at St. Elizabeth's?"

"Yes sir on the police band we've contacted the people assaulting that location."

"Who are they?" asked Stamper.

"They're a group of citizens, police, and firemen," answered the com tech.

"Is anyone in command there?"

"Yes sir a Lisa Edwards. She's with the Washington FD and everyone there says she's in command."

"Get her on the horn," ordered General Stamper.

"Yes sir," responded the com tech.

"Hello this is Lisa Edwards who am I speaking with?"

"This is General Stamper and I've been appointed by the President to take command of the assaults in Washington."

"I'm glad to hear the President made it out alive," said Lisa.

"This isn't President Obonyo. He was killed in the first assault. This is the new President Parker, and she has told me to take command of these assaults and that is what I'm doing" answered the General.

"All right General what do we do?"

"Ms. Edwards are you a vet?"

"Yes sir I was in the Air Force for twelve years as a fire tech. I served in the Sand Box and the Stan."

"All right I'm calling you to active duty as of

right now. I'm promoting you to the rank of Colonel and I'm putting you in charge of the battle at St. Elizabeth's. Is that understood?" said Stamper.

"Yes sir but I was only an E-8."

"I don't care. You're a bird colonel now and you're in command. I'll send everything your way as soon as I can. What's your situation on the ground now?"

"Sir we've taken most of the perimeter, some Apaches showed up out of nowhere and took out the enemy's Abrams, and now we're now into the buildings," answered Lisa.

"Good work! Take the fight to these terrorists and wipe them out."

"We will sir!"

"Remember Lisa you're in command" reminded General Stamper."

Having coordinated all four assaults Stamper broadcast an open call for any and all units of the United States military moving into or towards DC to contact him immediately. After almost a day of defeat and then of scattered responses finally the combined might of the United States was preparing to fall like a ton of bricks on the ISIS invaders as they headed towards one battle for the capital.

CHAPTER TWENTY-FIVE

Small Town America in the Crosshairs

In Baltimore, Richmond, and Harrisburg the loss of life from the corporate jets hitting major hospitals was horrendous. The fires raged and strained the capacity of the respective departments. However they were all in essence contained events. They caused confusion and led the governors of Virginia, Maryland, and Pennsylvania to refuse the initial order to give the federal government control over their State National Guards because they all waited for the next shoe to drop.

In the four towns where the National Guard Armories formed the springboards for the four ISIS Strike Forces the situations were much more complex and fluid.

In all four locations in addition to the city

police headquarters, airports, and oil depots had also been seized. Once they took everything they could from the four oil depots the terrorists set them ablaze causing massive fires that quickly spread to surrounding buildings and in most cases consumed whole neighborhoods.

Each airport was lightly defended; however, in every location the fuel reserves were set to explode and each building was wired with booby-traps and demolition charges.

At each police station in the time between when the Strike Forces had pulled out and the nation was aware that an attack was underway the terrorists had expanded their area of control from the police stations to larger areas several blocks in diameter. These areas were defended by Warriors in every building on their perimeters, snipers on every roof, and all the buildings were rigged with booby-traps and explosives. The tactical vehicles and equipment of the police departments were deployed and the streets were blocked with vehicles.

Such were the situations faced in three States. In each State the initial response was by state police augmented by surrounding local departments until the National Guards could be brought in which proved to be necessary in all four locations.

Maryland State Patrol Lieutenant, Nick Salvador had known Trooper Ron Rousseau since they were kids. They grew up in Cumberland, lived in the same subdivision, and went to the same schools. They had joined the National Guard together, deployed together, and they both joined the State Police at the same time and went through the academy together. They had drifted apart stationed in different areas of the state, but when they were both transferred to District Seven it was as if they had never been apart.

Now Nick was on a mission. He was determined to kill as many of these terrorists as he could. He wanted to do it for Ron. It just stuck in his craw, Ron didn't deserve to die like that, roasted alive in his patrol car.

Slowing down the response were the snipers who had been deployed as part of Phase Three. Resources were spread thin as police all over the State responded and often had prolonged gun battles with teams of highly trained, well-armed, and very accurate ISIS terrorist in rural settings.

By the time Nick was able to concentrate his

district's response to the terrorist hold on Rockville, the Maryland State Police had been taken over by the Federal Government and were under direct orders from President Parker to end all ISIS occupation immediately. As his officers concentrated in Rockville the West Virginia Guard began rolling through.

Using the radio the convoy was fully vetted and confirmed to be in fact an American unit and not another one under terrorist control. As the first vehicles of the convoy reached the Rockville exit they were contacted, "This is Lieutenant Salvador of the Maryland State Police come in West Virginia 13th."

Taking the microphone of the field radio from his communications tech Colonel Johnson answered, "This is Colonel Johnson of the West Virginia 13th Armored Brigade go ahead Lieutenant Salvador."

"Colonel we could use your help. We have terrorists holding a police station and an airport."

"Sorry no can do. We're on our way to Washington for a top priority mission."

"I understand about the priority situation Colonel."

"Sorry we couldn't stop to help. Good luck."

"Thanks Colonel."

As the State police from several districts augmented by the local PD from Aspen Hill, North Potomac, and Derwood began to surround the perimeter of the Montgomery County PD and the Rockville Municipal Airport they began taking fire from snipers both on the perimeter and dispersed outside the perimeter. The gathering police presence began to fill the surrounding streets with targets and dozens were killed and wounded by the snipers.

Salvador set up his headquarters in an Armored Mobile Command Post (AMCP) that had been given to his district by the Department of Defense.

"The first thing we need to do is neutralize the snipers who are outside the perimeter," Salvador ordered the State police SWAT team into action. One by one they located and silenced the snipers outside the perimeters, first around the police Station and then around the airport.

While these operations were underway Salvador had one of his men do a search of local resources looking for anyone who might have either helicopters or private planes that weren't at the municipal airport. "Sir we've located three crop duster services that have aircraft at independent fields in this area," came the report from Sargent Sarah Thomas, Salvador's second-in-command.

"Good work Sarah. Send teams to all three of them. Commandeer the aircraft, recruit the pilots, then have the team leaders report to me."

Turning to Sargent Ashaam Ahuja, Chief of Technical Operations for the Central Districts of the Maryland State Police, Salvador asked, "Sargent do we have any drones that can give us a view of what's inside that perimeter?"

"Yes Sir we have four drones with video capabilities."

"Great. Get them aloft ASAP and have the images sent to these monitors," Salvador ordered pointing over his shoulder to the long row of monitors that lined one side of the AMCP.

"Yes Sir," said Sargent Ahuja as he turned to accomplish his task.

"Lieutenant the Tactical Vehicles have just arrived from our main garage at Post 710. Other tactical vehicles are also arriving from

Derwood and Aspen Hill," Sargent Thomas reported.

"Have those vehicles deployed immediately. What've we got Sarah?"

"Counting our own we have half a dozen armored SWAT vehicles with their full complement of weapons and team members; we have four armored cars, two with turrets and seven armored trucks with rams."

"All right there are four streets intersecting the enemy perimeter, two are on South Campus Drive and two are Mannakee Street. I want one armored car blocking each one. As soon as we get Intel we'll figure out how to proceed."

Sargent Ahuja reported, "Sir we have visuals from the drones."

Salvador walked over and looked at the screens showing the video feed from the State Police drones.

"Look at that," Lieutenant Salvador said pointing at one of the screens. "Do you see that?"

Following Salvador's finger Sargent Wilkins the head of the District SWAT teams said, "It looks like they left the south side of the perimeter along Mannakee Street with fewer defenses in depth than anywhere else." Pointing at the screen, Wilkins continued, "Look at that, there's only one other road block between the initial two car road block at the perimeter and the station house."

"Maybe it's a trap?'" interjected Sargent Thomas.

"Or maybe they just ran out of vehicles to use," said Wilkins.

"So what do you think? Should we choose that as our point of entry?" Salvador asked.

"I say we go for it," Wilkins said.

When Salvador heard nothing further from his trusted second-in-command he asked, "Sarah what do you think?'

"I think these guys are way too sophisticated, and this whole thing has been planned out far too well for this to be an oversight. I think it's a trap."

Looking at the screens and then looking at both of his subordinates Salvador was struggling with how to form up for what was going to be a military type assault. During this time there was an almost constant arrival of more and more police. Soon Salvador and his team were joined in the AMCP by the police chiefs of Aspen Hill, North Potomac, and Derwood. Also present were Lieutenant Bob Graining the commander of the neighboring State Police District. his second-in-command, and his head of SWAT.

They all discussed the situation and the majority of them decided to push into the enemy area along what appeared to be the street with the least road blocks, the path of least resistance.

"Lieutenant Salvador the air teams are assembled," reported Sargent Ahuja.

"What've we got, Sargent?"

"There are two helicopters and four light planes."

"All right I want them to get airborne now and come in for air support. Have them report in as soon as they reach the area."

"Yes sir!" Ahuja responded as he turned back to the troopers at the communications desks.

Trying one more time to get her lone warning heard Sargent Thomas said, "I still think this is a trap. These guys are way to savvy to leave such a glaring weakness in their defenses."

Before anyone could respond the sound of a tremendous explosion was heard in the enclosed AMCP above all the din of the communications center and the conversation of the gathered police leaders.

"What was that?" "Holy crap!" "My God!" were some of the exclamations from the gathered leaders.

"Sir it's just been reported that the Airport has erupted in a massive explosion. The team there had battled their way into the terminal and the hangers and just as they reached the tower the whole place went up; the terminal, the hangers, the fuel depot everything all at once," Sargent Abdul Ahuja reported.

"How many officers were in those buildings?" asked Salvador.

"They're reporting at least a hundred were in the buildings and several dozen more were close enough to feel the full force of the explosions. The AMCP there is reporting casualties including injured will be at least two hundred."

"I think we should hold off on any assault until the military gets here," Thomas said hoping that maybe now they would listen to her.

The thought of all those dead and injured officers, the thoughts of so many dead and dying friends drove any hesitation out of Lieutenant Salvador and the rest of the leadership. They were now more eager than ever to get at these murders polluting their cherished America.

"Let's get these sons-a-bitches," said Daryl Edwards, Chief of the Aspen Hill PD and a former SEAL.

"I'm with Daryl. We've got the men and the equipment to take these killers down," added William "Big Bill" Jenkins, the Chief of the Derwood PD who was a father of five and whose oldest son was one of the officers at the airport.

With everyone in agreement now except Sargent Thomas the police leaders hurriedly prepared their assault on the Montgomery County PD station and the defensive area the terrorists had established.

"Have the men surrounding the perimeter keep up a constant fire from all directions," ordered Lieutenant Salvador.

"Let's send a diversionary attack down South

Campus Drive. That street ends right at the station house and they'll surely treat that as the most serious threat," added Chief Edwards.

"Have the diversionary attack start before the main attack," was Lieutenant Graining's contribution.

"We'll need to make the diversionary attack look credible," interjected Chief Jorkowskey from North Potomac.

"Beside the armored car already on South Campus have ten or twelve patrol cars form up to lead the diversionary assault and send at least fifty officers on foot. That should look convincing. Sargent Ahuja, contact the officer in command on South Campus and tell him to form up and make it as visible as possible."

"Yes sir!'

Turning to Lieutenant Graining, Salvador said, "Bob I want you to take command of the diversionary attack."

"All right Nick. I'll make it as convincing as possible"

Calling out to Sargent Ahuja, "Tell the air support to sweep the roofs and keep them clear. Also tell them to take any targets of opportunity they see."

"Yes sir!"

Looking at the rest of the police leaders Nick said, "All right men go out and form up your officers for the main assault. Bring every vehicle we have around to head north on Mannakee Street into the south side of their perimeter. Get every man we have who isn't engaged blocking one of the other streets to keep the snipers busy or involved in the diversionary attack. We want our main assault to be overwhelming," Salvador told the assembled leaders.

As they were leaving Salvador pulled Sargent Wilkins aside, "How're the SWAT Teams deployed?"

"We have one on each side of the perimeter and one on each street entrance. All the rest are being held in reserve."

"I want everyone in reserve to join in this main assault. I want them leading us in and I also want a team at the rear of the column for mop up."

Perhaps Sargent Wilkins was the only one who had given much thought to Sargent Thomas' warnings, though he hadn't spoken up or supported her in any way, now voiced a note of caution, "What about booby traps? What if they have everything rigged to come down on us once we're in?"

"They probably do but we can't wait around and let these no-good savages hold even an inch of American soil when we're here armed and ready to take it back," answered Salvador. For the first time in his long and distinguished career with the Maryland State Police Lieutenant Nick Salvador let his emotions get the best of him.

Usually he was a cool head in any situation. Maybe it was losing his best friend Ron. Maybe it was the feelings of responsibility for losing so many officers under his command at the airport. Maybe it was just the rising blood of a trained warrior in the face of a mighty battle. Whatever it was Salvador threw advice and caution to the winds when he looked his old friend Nat Wilkins in the eyes and quoted one of his boyhood heroes, David Farragut when he said, "Damn the torpedoes, full speed ahead."

Being a loyal subordinate and a brave leader Nick answered, "Yes sir!" and then left the AMCP to order his troops for the main assault.

Moments later Sargent Ahuja announced that

the air support had arrived. Nick was about to order the diversionary assault to begin when he was interrupted by Sargent Ahuja, "Sir I've just been contacted by the 11th Armored Brigade of the West Virginia National Guard. He says they have been ordered to come to Rockville and take over the assault on the Montgomery County PD station house."

"Did they say when they'll arrive?"

"They said ETA of about two hours."

The thought of leaving the terrorists who had killed so many good officers, who had helped bring about an invasion of his beloved America, was too much. Nick didn't even hesitate as he keyed the microphone that hung from his left shoulder and said, "South Campus Drive, it's a go."

Calling out to his second-in-command Sargent Sarah Thomas, "Sarah you stay in AMCP and coordinate the communications with Ashaam" Lieutenant Nick Salvador stepped out to lead the main assault himself. As he stepped out of the large armored vehicle Nick couldn't help but feel as if he was stepping into History, as if he was about to fulfill his destiny, and that all his life and training had led him to this moment, to this assault. He couldn't think past it. He had nothing on his mind except to accomplish his task, take back the station house, and restore American honor and sovereignty.

The strategy appeared to be working. The assault teams coming up South Campus Drive out of the Montgomery College campus met with such heavy resistance that they stalled out in front of the barricades of burned out vehicles across the street. The enemy fire from the perimeter buildings was so intense the suppressing fire of the SWAT team was ineffective and the enemy fire was forcing the SWAT members themselves to stay under cover.

As soon as it seemed like the assault down South Campus Drive had fully engaged the enemy, using a large Armored Car with a snow plow as a ram on the front to lead the assault Salvador ordered, "Attack!" Immediately the entire convoy of vehicles started heading north on Mannakee Street. Just as planned the rams on the leading vehicles were able to shove the two blocking cars aside and the entire column advance straight on the station house. Officers were fanning out moving into the lower floors of the surrounding buildings. The enemy fire was light and the SWAT teams using suppressing fire appeared to have the enemy bottled up.

"Come on we caught them napping," called Nick into his microphone as he and the squad of men in his armored car exited the vehicle to lead the assault into the station house.

Using an AR-15 on full auto Nick emptied a magazine on a window in the second floor of the station house and was in the act of reloading when all hell broke loose.

Remotely detonated booby-traps went off in the ground floors of all the surrounding buildings as masses of terrorists came rushing down the stairways quickly killing any of the stunned or wounded police who had survived the blasts.

From positions on the roofs FIM-92 Stingers were launched and every helicopter and plane was soon falling from the sky to add another explosion, another fire, and more death to an already hellish scene in Rockville, Maryland.

Simultaneously Warriors with RPGs fired on the armored vehicles setting each one ablaze as shaped shells punctured their relatively light armor and killed all within. While all this mayhem was exploding all around them the men of the main assault came under a withering cross fire from numerous machine guns which had been hidden from view.

The diversionary assault coming down South Campus Street was receiving the same treatment and was being decimated in its tracks.

Within moments what seemed like a looming victory turned into a stunning defeat. Through the dust raised by the many explosions Lieutenant Nick Salvador watched as his officers were falling like wheat before a combine as the expertly placed machine guns turned Rockville's once peaceful Mannakee Street into America's version of the killing fields.

Nick had been knocked down by the concussion of the initial blasts. Then he had been hit by flying shrapnel when the armored car he had been in exploded. The fire was scorching him as he lay bleeding and dazed behind some wreckage from one of the buildings.

Trying to collect his thoughts Nick could see that he and his officers were pinned down by the machine guns. RPGs were also being launched at pockets of resistance. "If we don't get out of here we're all going to die," Nick said to himself. Keying his microphone he called out, "Withdraw! Withdraw! Retreat!"

He could see a few groups nearest to the entrance of the defensive perimeter try to break cover and retreat. They were all cut down almost instantly. None of them made it out. As seconds seemed like hours and moments like days no one else moved. From where he lay Nick could see the body of Chief Edwards and Chief Jorkowskey. "We've got to get out of here," Nick thought as he heard jumbles of radio traffic knowing his plan had collapsed in upon them and was buried under the superior firepower and tactics of the enemy.

Watching as more and more died as bullets smashed and crashed all about him Nick knew he had to lead the way. Jumping from cover Nick cried into his radio, "Come on let's go fo…." Which was all he got out before his body was almost torn in two by a cross fire hurricane of machine guns from several locations.

Between the RPGs, the machine guns, and the snipers it wasn't long until almost all of the assaulting police were either dead or incapacitated.

In the AMCP Sargent Thomas fought to see through the tears as she thought, "If only they would've listened. If only they'd waited for the military."

"Ashaam, tell everyone to pull back. Have all remaining officers join the teams that are surrounding the perimeter. Tell them to keep up their fire. We need to hold these animals in place till the military get here," Sarah said.

As word spread through the police community of south central Maryland whole departments kept showing up and soon there were hundreds of officers on all sides pouring a withering fire into the defensive perimeter around the Montgomery County PD station house in Rockville. Almost every one of them had lost friends and even relatives in the failed assault or at the airport. With personal and professional rage they fired round after round trying to hit anyone anything just trying to make a difference to help Americans re-take America from these terrorist invaders.

About forty-five minutes after the failed assault the 11th Armored Brigade started arriving. In short order under the command of Colonel Hank Osborn the Apache's and Abrams of the 11th Armored reduced the entire defensive area around the Montgomery County PD station house into a smoking crater.

His men walked through the wreckage looking for any civilian survivors. There were none. They looked for surviving police from either the station house or the assaults. They found a few from the assaults buried under debris, wounded, and shell shocked. There were none from the station house. Against orders many terrorists who survived were shot when they were found. A few tried to resist, most were too badly wounded to resist but they were shot anyway. A few, a very few were taken as captives.

By mid-afternoon of the attack Rockville, Maryland though under a sky turned black from the many fires, though filled with destroyed buildings, vehicles, homes, and lives, though choked with the dead and dying was once again free of terrorists. What they would never be free of was the terror.

Reproduced three more times with varying degrees of similarity in Calverton, Maryland; Bristol, Maryland; and Vienna, Virginia battles raged and people died as Americans shook free of the invaders our own leaders had brought into our land. The Romans had brought in the Goths, the Vandals, and the Franks. In like manner the ideologues of the Obonyo

Administration had ignored the wishes of the people and imported an army of American-hating Jihadists whose sole objective was to drive a sword into our leader's bleeding heart.

CHAPTER TWENTY-SIX

Victory at Any Cost

Having taken over the office of the base commander President Parker was in conference with General Ed Brown, her Chairman of the Joint Chiefs. They were pouring over the latest satellite and AWACS photos when a Lieutenant from the Communications Center knocked and entered. "Madam President, here is a message from Admiral Davis," handing a single slip of paper to the President.

It said, "Fighters and bombers from the Fifth and the Sixth Fleets have hit Raqqa and every ISIS oil terminal and shipping point. The first wave has returned to their carriers and the second wave is on the way. Between the waves Tomahawk cruise missiles were launched and have hit every known ISIS military installation in their territory."

As the lieutenant left, the President said, "Get me the latest information on the four towns under attack and get me the overall commander of the battle in Washington on the horn."

"Yes Ma'am," the Lieutenant said sharply as he left to carry out his orders.

"That's some good news Madam President. It feels good to finally hit these terrorists where they live. For months I've been hearing how we were dropping more leaflets telling the Jihadis we were going to bomb them than we dropped bombs. I think I can speak for everyone in the services that it feels good to have a Commander-in-Chief who isn't afraid to command" said General Brown.

"Who did you finally find to take command back there General?" asked the President.

General Brown answered, "I promoted Colonel Rick Stamper, the commander of the Delta Team in the North Atlantic Military Division to Brigadier and gave him overall command. He had already organized his Delta team and several SEAL teams from Hampton Roads and led an attack on one of the hospitals. I've looked over his service record, and if I could have picked him myself I don't think we could've found a better man for the job."

"That's what we want. Self-starters and people who want to bring the fight to the enemy. Get that new General on the horn. I want to talk to him," said the President. Mike Bender immediately left to relay her order to the communications room.

"Your orders are being carried out all along the line. The Apache formations have intervened effectively and multiple National Guard units are moving towards Washington as we speak," replied General Brown.

Another currier from the Communications Center knocked and entered, "Madam President, a message from General Corbaine the Commanding General of the West Virginia National Guard," handing the message to the President, and waiting at attention for a reply.

Looking at the message President Parker read it to General Brown, "The 11th Armored Brigade has liberated Rockville, Maryland. There have been mass casualties among the police and the civilians. There were minimal casualties among the military. Most of the terrorists have been killed and few have been taken prisoner."

"Lieutenant get me the current information on

the other three towns occupied by the enemy."

"Yes Ma'am," answered the Lieutenant. He then turned and left the room to carry out his orders.

"It looks like things are coming back from the brink," President Parker said as she returned to her study of the Intel photos.

At the same time as another currier from the Communications Center knocked and walked into the office Mike Bender also came in. Before the currier could say anything Mike stepped up to the President and said quietly in her ear, "Madam President could I have a moment alone."

"Give us the room please."

General Brown and the currier stepped out of the room. "Please close the door," the President said as General Brown stepped out. Once the door was closed the President asked, "All right Mike what is it?"

"There's a radio station in Janesville, Wisconsin that's reporting that Speaker Bryan is alive and being held incommunicado. The Governor of Wisconsin is saying the same thing" said Mike.

Without hesitation she responded, "On my

direct authority order the Wisconsin National Guard to arrest the Governor and hold him in isolation. And order the Wisconsin State Police to shut that radio station down."

"Madam President do you really think that the American people are going to stand for all this?"

"Mike you're either with me or you're against me. Which is it?"

"I'm with you Madam President. I just thought you might want to take a moment to think about all this before it gets completely out of hand."

The President looked Mike in the eye and said, "There's nothing to think about Mike we're under attack. There are savages holding American territory in the middle of our own capital. They've killed our President and almost our entire command and control both civilian and military. I'm taking the actions that will restore our control over our own territory and I'm moving to destroy these ISIS animals for once and for all. I have no doubt that the American people will stand behind what I've done."

"But Madam President the line of succession is clear and it's blackletter law."

Narrowing her gaze President Parker said, "We need victory at any cost. We cannot afford to waver or falter by one iota in the face of this cowardly and unprovoked attack. I am not about to stand down and cause even more confusion by trying to explain what I've done or allow these political hacks to step in and foul things up. It's because of them that we're in this situation to begin with. So, Mike, this is the last time I'm going to say this, you're either with me or you're against me. Which is it Mike? Are you going to do your job or does someone else need to do it?"

Mike had been with Patricia Parker since they were in the military together and he was her adjutant. He followed her into civilian life in the corporate world and then into politics. For more than twenty years he had been her right-hand man, and no matter what his qualms he was not about to leave her side now. "I'm with you Madam President. I'll convey your orders to the Wisconsin National Guard and the State Police immediately."

"Good. I knew you wouldn't leave me Mike. We've got a war to win so let's get it going."

"Yes Ma'am," Mike said as he walked to the door and opened it to leave.

"Mike, tell General Brown to come back and send in the runner from the Communications Center" added the President as she turned back to study the maps and pictures on the conference table.

"Yes, Ma'am."

General Brown re-entered the room followed by two runners from the Communications Center.

As the General joined the President at the table the two runners handed their messages to the President.

One said, "The Maryland National Guard report that both Calverton and Bristol have been secured. Units are helping with relief and rescue in those locations. Other units are moving towards Washington."

The other said, "The Virginia National Guard report that the enemy troops in Vienna have been neutralized and several brigades have been dispatched to Washington."

"Dismissed," said the President. Both runners left the room. Then she continued, "General this thing is pulling together."

Another runner stuck his head in the door and

said, "President, the commanding General of the Washington assaults is on the horn, line one."

"General put him on speaker," President Parker said.

Grabbing a phone off his desk and placing it in the middle of the big conference table General Brown intimately familiar with the equipment in what had been his office for several years, pushed a button and instantly they were connected.

"General this is President Parker, what's happening on the ground in Washington?"

"Ma'am this is General Stamper, at Walter Reed. We have an armored brigade of the West Virginia National Guard. They're actively engaging the enemy and making steady progress. At Adventist Healthcare my joint task force of Delta Force and SEALS are spear heading the assault and they're fighting room-to-room taking back the buildings. At St. Elizabeth the attacking force is made up of Washington PD, Washington FD, and civilians. I've appointed a Fireman with military experience as a Colonel and given her overall command of the battle there. These minutemen have taken the perimeter of the complex without any help and now that the Apaches have arrived they're storming the buildings. At the Virginia Hospital Center a network of militia groups from Virginia have assaulted the complex. Their leader is a twenty year vet. I've appointed him a colonel and given him command of the battle there."

"Good work General," said the President. "We have multiple resources on the way to you. Whatever they are and whoever is in command as soon as they enter DC they are under your command. I don't give a damn about seniority or rank. You're in command in DC. These orders have been transmitted from here but if anyone gives you any crap you tell them to contact General Ed Brown."

"Yes Ma'am."

"Keep the pressure on the enemy and take back the capitol."

"Yes Ma'am."

The President reached out and hung up the phone.

"Madam President I have to ask you a question" said General Brown

Without looking up from the Intel pictures

President Parker said, "What is it General?"

"Ma'am I have been told that you are holding the Speaker of the House in custody. Is that true?"

Standing erect and looking the General dead in the eye the President said, "That is true. He didn't surface until after I was sworn in and had taken command here at Fort Huachuca. I'd already made my appointments to command and started the offensive. It is my opinion that once the oath of office has been taken the office has been filled. In addition I didn't think the country needed another break in command in one day. So I ordered the Speaker held in protective custody until this crisis is over."

The General just stood there looking at the woman he had been obeying and working with for most of the day. The woman he had believed was the legally designated President of the United States. The look on his face was one of confusion and worry.

"General this crisis was caused by the political class that has seized power in this country through a combination of voter fraud, voter apathy, and gerrymandering. These Progressive hacks have ignored the public.

Against the advice of anyone who loves America and wants to keep it the number one nation on Earth imported these terrorists. They have sacrificed our best and brightest on the altar of their vanities in battles around the world they start and won't allow us to finish. I have no intention of handing over power to the very people who have brought this hell upon us."

Taking a step towards the General she continued, "If you think you should remove me from power and surrender this battle on the verge of victory go ahead and release the author of the Great Betrayal and watch as he tries to negotiate his way out of this."

Knowing that his next step would define the rest of his life and career General Brown thought about what he should say.

"General, you are either with me or against me, which is it?"

"Madam President, I agree with you. Once the oath of office has been given you entered into the office and I also agree that the country does not need and cannot endure another change in leadership in the midst of this crisis."

Moving forward as if they hadn't just faced and passed a crucial moment in the nation's History

President Parker ordered her Chairman of the Joint Chiefs, "Have the enemy prisoners handed over to the Defense Intelligence Agency ASAP. I want any actionable information we can gain any way we can get it. Nothing is off the table. Get those Jihadis talking before another shoe drops."

Another runner from the Communications Center knocked at the door and entered. "General Brown we have an urgent message from the Division Chief of the Border Patrol in Arizona," handing him the message.

Reading aloud the General shared the message with the President, "To General Edward Brown Commanding Fort Huachuca: General a large force of ISIS terrorists, cartel battle formations, MS-13 gangs, and what can only be described as either Mexican Army units or terrorists in Mexican uniforms with heavy weapons and vehicles from the Mexican Army have broken through the border east of Nogales. They wiped out our border guards, the police officers, and sheriff's deputies who were helping us hold them back and they are heading in your direction. They number at least ten thousand strong; they have military grade weapons, military vehicles including armored cars, more than a dozen tanks, and at least 6 M110 Self-Propelled Howitzers: From Division Chief Thomas Skleer."

Looking at each other neither said a word for a moment. Than the President asked, "Have any of the Guard units arrived yet?"

"A few small ones have straggled in. None with armor. We'll be hard pressed to withstand a full assault. We just don't have that many troops. Most of our personnel are specialists and command officers," General Brown answered.

"Contact General Zchevinsky at Davis–Monthan Air Force Base and tell him to send enough fighters to annihilate these gate crashers" said the President.

"Ma'am if they are moving forward at full speed they could be on top of us in less than an hour. We could be in range of those M110 Self-Propelled Howitzers in ten to fifteen minutes which will be long before the Air Force is on top of them. By the time the air force gets here we could be overrun."

"I guess we will just have to brace for impact, keep our heads down, and do our job then. Send all personnel not involved here in command and control to the southern perimeter. I mean cooks, MPs, secretaries, everyone who can carry a gun," ordered the President.

General Brown admired the courage and decisiveness of the new Commander-in-Chief, and he realized that whether or not she was going to remain president when this was all over she was certainly the president America needed right now. However as her only military advisor he felt duty bound to give her cautionary counsel, "Madam President this location could become completely untenable very quickly. I have to counsel that we withdraw immediately up Highway 90 and take I-10 to Tuscan. We should be able to stay out of range until the Air Force can deal with these raiders."

"General, America has been knocked back on our heels but I'll be damned if the President of the United States is going to turn tail and run from Mexican bandits and ISIS scum on American Soil. I won't hear of it! We will soldier on and let the Air Force take these invaders out."

"Yes Ma'am!" said General Brown as he prepared to stand beside the woman he had gambled his career on, the only person he believed had a chance of salvaging this situation and righting America's listing ship of state.

Pivoting back to where she was before the latest runner brought news of the Mexican invasion President Parker said to her personal assistant, "Mike get in touch with whoever is holding those prisoners and tell them they have my authorization to use any means necessary to get them talking ASAP. I want some Intel about what is going on in those buildings."

CHAPTER TWENTY-SEVEN

The Battle of Arlington

Up Close and Personal

Mitch lay behind the shattered chassis of a Bradley. He and Blake Simmons his radio man were surrounded by about twenty members of the Dinwiddie Patriots. Some were wounded, all were smudged with dirt, and grease, and blood. The black smoke of burning diesel and rubber tinged with the stink of human flesh hung over the space between the perimeter of the Virginia Hospital Center and the shattered building which had once been the pride of Arlington.

Mitch and his group fought their way one foot at a time in the face of 50 caliber machine guns from the Abrams and concentrated fire from the snipers in the buildings. The area was strewn with both American and ISIS dead. "This is about as far as we can get. There's still twenty to thirty yards of open space with no cover between us and the buildings and we'll never make it with those 50s knocking down anything that moves," Mitch said as he realized they may not make it into the buildings after all the sacrifice the Patriots had already made.

"Maybe if we ordered every group that's pinned down along the line to rush them at once," suggested Ed Eastman Mitch's lifelong friend.

"I think that would just end up with all of us dying Ed," answered Mitch.

Mitch's squad watched as a young man broke cover about ten yards to their left and managed to dodge the enemy fire as he ran, jumped, and rolled until he made one last leap and landed in the crater they were currently occupying. It was Billy Hill a member of Mitch's son Junior's squad. Mitch had known Billy since he and Junior started hanging out in high school. Mitch had always liked him, he was a decent person and one of the best mechanics Mitch had ever known.

"Hey Billy," Ed said.

Not taking time for any personal greetings or small talk Billy said, "Our radio was hit a while back. Junior wants you to know he has more than a dozen men, and he will follow your lead."

"You stay here Billy. There's no need for you to try to get back with the message that we aren't moving from here."

Mitch was frustrated as were all the rest of the Patriots. They had come so far and sacrificed so much. Each and every one of them wanted to close with the enemy. They wanted to clean this nest of terrorists out, kill every one of them, and raise an American flag from the roof. But they all knew that without anything powerful enough to silence those Abrams and their 50s they were stumped.

Inside the conference room Tamam Udail the commander of Strike Force Four had just been informed that the perimeter was now completely in the hands of the Americans. "Sadad, it is time to release some of the Unbeliever whores so that after we have sent most of these Americans to Hell and we have gone to Paradise they will know how we have humiliated them," Tamam said to his second in command.

"I will make it so," replied Sadad turning immediately to the radio man and ordering him to have the guards release about fifty of the captive women.

"Kill all the other whores and order our patrols to kill all the patients" Tamam ordered Luqman Ghazwan his cousin and the commander of his guards and interior patrols.

"As you command. Not one of these polluted Unbeliever dogs will escape the wrath of Allah," answered Luqman who passed the orders on to his men using the microphone that dangled from his left shoulder.

"Hey Mitch, look at this," Betty Lynn Taylor called out from the north side of the position.

Mitch looked at Betty Lynn and couldn't help but marvel. Here was this little 5'2" mother of three dressed in fatigues, covered in mud and blood holding an AR-15 risking her life to attack the invaders. "There is a real Patriot," Mitch thought as he crawled over to Betty's position to take a look.

"Hold your fire! Hold your fire!" Mitch yelled as loud as he could. Then he said to Don Patterson, the man who owned and operated the jewelry shop next to his gun store and one of the founding members of the Dinwiddie patriots, "Well what do you make of that?" as he stared at an ISIS Warrior in American army fatigues waving a white flag as he stepped out of the shattered front doors of the hospital.

"I never thought these suicide pot lickers would ever surrender," said Don.

The silence was almost deafening as all the Patriot groups close enough to see the man with the flag stopped firing. The firing from the building had also stopped and as word spread by radio to cease fire the sudden return to a level of noise close to what had always been normal until today seemed to come as a crash of stillness in a crumbling world.

Blake yelled out to Mitch, "The guys on the other side are reporting a man with a white flag has come out of the building over there too."

In perfect English and with no accent at all the man with the flag called out, "Don't shoot. We are sending out some of your women."

Immediately a group of about twenty-five or thirty women came out. Those that could ran towards the Americans. Some were naked, others were only partially clothed. Some were barely able to walk and were being helped by others.

"I thought these animals would kill all their hostages," said Betty Lynn.

"I did too," and "Praise God they're showing a little humanity after all," were some of the other comments in the crater Mitch's group currently called home.

As soon as the women were safely in the crater the fire from the buildings and the 50s opened up with a vengeance killing and wounding several people who had gotten careless and exposed themselves as the women came out. It didn't take long, just a moment or two for the horrific story of what had happened to the woman to fill the Patriots with rage, and as the news spread around the ring of fire that surrounded the buildings the level of hate and the thirst for revenge rose to unbelievable heights.

As all of this was transpiring on ground level a possible game changer was brewing in a little used corridor not far from the conference room the invaders had chosen for their headquarters. There the team of employees, visitors, and a few doctors, led by Chelsea the pharmaceutical sales rep, prepared to do what they could to help the assault they could hear going on downstairs.

They had successfully over powered a few two man teams of Warriors on patrol as they made their way from the tunnels to the top floor. This had increased their arsenal by four AR-15s, four pistols, four knives, and another dozen hand grenades. It had also increased their confidence and made them ready for the fight.

Back in the conference room Tamam Udail raising his voice to be heard by all over the rising din of battle called out, "Brothers this has been a glorious day of victory for our beloved Caliph and for Allah! We have brought death and destruction to the dark heart of the Great Satan. We have brought shame and misery upon their heads. And we have delivered such punishment and humiliation upon the Unbeliever empire of the west that they will follow their sin and unbelief to the Grand Battle of Deraa where the prophet Himself, peace be upon him, will lead the armies of the Believers to final victory, and the Mahdi shall rid the world of evil."

Shouts of "Allah Akbar! Allah Akbar!" filled the room.

"You have accomplished this already. All that remains is for us to die a glorious martyr's death and find our sweet reward in Paradise. I will see you in Paradise this day my brothers and we wi...." Was as far as Tamam got when two doors crashed open and he had a hurried view of a tall woman throwing a grenade into the room. The first one was followed quickly by dozens more. The blast took out the whole room.

Failing to get either door closed before the first grenades began exploding the blowback from the shrapnel and the concussion from the ensuing mega multi-blasts instantly killed Chelsea, Doctor Tom, and Doctor Ed. Several others were severely wounded. As those who could ran for the back stairs that had brought them up from the tunnels they were intercepted by ISIS patrols running from both ends of the corridor. In a hail of gunfire the Americans managed to take out more than a dozen Warriors but eventually all resistance ceased as the last American, one of the janitors was finally brought down with a shot to the head.

After the women had come out Mitch, like every other Patriot, was straining at the bit to get at the enemy, but they were still pinned down with no way to move forward.

"I guess we're just going to have to hold our positions until the cavalry arrives," Mitch said to no one in particular. Then he said, "Pass the word we hold in place with minimum exposure. Tell the troops to conserve their ammo in case they try a breakout and tell them to keep their heads down." Blake immediately began transmitting the orders.

Suddenly there was a tremendous explosion on the top floor of the hospital. Glass and a few bodies flew out to come crashing down in the no-man's land between the Patriot positions and the buildings.

"What the hell was that!" exclaimed Ed as he threw himself to the ground.

"Maybe it was an airstrike," Billy offered.

"No. It looks like something blew up inside," said Mitch.

"It sure does. If it had been a missile from the outside I doubt if any bodies or glass would have been blown out," added Don.

"I've seen what Hellfire missiles and 105s can do, and that explosion wasn't that big," said Ed.

"Whatever it was I hope it killed a whole bunch of those assholes," Billy said.

"Hey Mitch we're getting a call from a Colonel

Jenkins with the 30th Attack Reconnaissance Battalion," said Blake.

"Give me the headset," Mitch said as he crawled over to the radio position.

Once he had the headset on Mitch said, "Come in Colonel Jenkins."

"Is this Colonel Williams?"

Hearing it for the first time made Mitch feel strange, but he had taken General Stamper's orders to heart and he was determined to answer the call.

"Yes, this is Colonel Williams."

"Colonel Williams I'll be in firing range of your location in about two minutes. What do you want us to do?"

As a former captain giving orders to a colonel didn't come natural but Mitch was a born leader and he carried the weight of a field promotion and a general behind him so without a thought about it he took to it like a duck takes to water, "Colonel we're pinned down by the Abrams the terrorists have backed right into the hospital buildings. If you can take them out we'll be able to start the final assault."

"Will do Colonel. Tell your people to keep their heads down and we'll have those tanks out of action in about three minutes," Colonel Jenkins replied.

"Great." answered Mitch. Turning to Blake he said, "Tell everyone to keep their heads down. There'll be some incoming ordinance in about three minutes. As soon as the blast is over everyone rush the building. And tell them to avoid the openings the tanks have made. There'll be secondary explosions and fires."

"Yes Sir," Blake said and immediately sent out the message.

At the rear of the perimeter battle, hundreds of Americans from the surrounding neighborhoods had been coming up to see if they could help. The Patriots distributed weapons and formed them into squads each led by one of the members of the Virginia Patriots Network. By the time the missiles hit the tanks there were upwards of three thousand Americans armed and ready to take back their territory with more arriving constantly.

The detonations of the incoming Hellfire missiles were like the sound of a volcano erupting or what you would expect to hear as the doorbell of hell. The buildings slumped and sagged and in some places actually came down in crashing jangles of concrete and steel. Shards of glass, pieces of furniture, and parts of bodies rained down causing some injuries to the Patriots sheltering in the craters and behind the blasted vehicles that littered the property.

The dust was still in the air when Mitch yelled "Charge!" as he jumped up and led his squad straight towards the door that had not long ago served as the portal for the woman captives. The cry was echoed from the voices of hundreds of other squad leaders as the Patriots all climbed out of hiding and raced towards the buildings with one thought animating all of them, "Kill the invaders!"

The massed fire from the thousands of Patriots rushing the building was like a solid wall of lead clearing the path in front of them.

As Mitch led his men into the hospital through the front door they walked into a cross fire from several locations in the big lobby. Mitch dived behind some big metal planters. The plants had all been shot away but they provided some cover. "Over here," Mitch yelled as the rounds from the crossfire zoomed through the lobby. Most of the Patriots hit the floor and started returning fire.

Blake was on the floor next to Mitch and so was Ed. Don and Billy were behind the planters on the other side of the door. Betty Lynn lay in the middle of the door way the right side of her head a mass of blood where a round from an AR-15 had found its mark. Mitch threw up a hurried prayer for her family and tossed a grenade into one of the hallways that entered the lobby just beyond the big information desk. Before that first grenade exploded he had another in the air and he could see several more heading for hallways around the lobby.

Explosion followed explosion and the deadly crossfire stopped. Mitch was on his feet and again rushing deeper into the building with his squad following. Other squads were now piling in behind Mitch including the ones led by his son Jr. and the one led by his wife.

Just as Mitch came up to the big information desk two Jihadis jumped up and started firing on full auto into the room. A bullet grazed Mitch and sent him sprawling on the marble tiled floor. Next to him one round hit Don in the face and another hit him in the left shoulder sending him spinning spraying blood in all directions as he corkscrewed to the floor.

Several other members of Mitch's squad were hit along with others who had followed them in. Without breaking stride Billy jumped over the information desk taking down one of the gunmen. While he was falling on top of that one he fired a few rounds to his side and took out the other one. He landed with his full force on top of the Warrior knocking the breath out of him. Then grabbing his knife and plunging it into the man's throat keeping the breath from ever entering him again.

With blood running down the side of his face from the grazing wound Mitch got to his feet, went around the information desk, and helped Billy to his feet, "That was a brave thing to do Billy, I'm proud of you son," Mitch said.

Quickly assessing the situation Mitch called out, "You men on the right take those two corridors there. You on the left take the other two. Ed you stay here and keep the incoming troops dividing as evenly as possible between the two sides and this central corridor." Then he took off leading the Patriots in the middle down the large central corridor.

There was resistance but it was light and they lost a few as they killed many. As they entered areas where there were patient rooms they saw that all the patients had been killed.

The blood lust in all of them was rising more and more as they saw what the invaders had done to these innocent Americans.

As they were clearing the first floor there came a moment when after clearing a large meeting room Mitch realized that his beloved wife Joan and his son Junior were both in the room. Looking at each other across the bullet ridden conference table, the shattered furniture, and the many bodies strewn about they all tried to say, "I love you be safe," with their eyes before they rushed in different directions leading their squads to the battle none of them wanted and each of them was determined to win.

Once the first floor was secure Mitch sent several squads into each stairwell. Just as he was about to lead his own squad into one of the stairwells Blake said, "Colonel I've got a Major Detlefson of the 47th Infantry Virginia National Guard on the line."

"Taking the headset Mitch said, "Major Detlefson this is Colonel Williams what have you got for me?"

"Colonel my brigade is arriving on the scene what do you want us to do?"

"Surround the entire area and make sure none

of these ISIS terrorists escape. Send in
squads not needed for the outer perimeter to
help clear the building. Be aware the enemy is
in desert sand fatigues. Our people are all in
green camo, police uniforms, and civilian
clothes," Mitch said.

"Yes sir," Major Detlefson answered. For the
first time all day Mitch began to feel that
victory was certain.

Facing surprisingly light resistance Mitch led
the Patriots, police, civilians, and now U.S.
infantry up one floor and then after clearing
that up another. Floor-by-floor, room-by-room
they took back the Virginian Hospital Center
not knowing that the command center of the
terrorists was just a smoking ruin and that
they were facing a splintered and leaderless
rabble that had once been a cohesive fighting
force.

CHAPTER TWENTY-EIGHT

The Battle of St. Elizabeth:

Up the Down Stairwell

Lisa Billingham and Sargent Bushings rushed into the building firing into the faces of the enemy. Hundreds and soon thousands of police, firemen, and civilians poured into the buildings of St Elizabeth Hospital. They shot anything that moved. By force of numbers they pushed the defenders back from the windows and doors. Room by room sometimes desk by desk the fire fights raged leaving dead, wounded and dying scattered in every conceivable pose, piled on the floor, slumped over desks and chairs, and half in and half out of doors and windows. It was no exaggeration to say the building was littered with bodies. Still the Americans in their righteous anger assaulted the enemy with a ferocity they had never imagined.

Then suddenly all the Warriors withdrew to the stairwells. The crash of the 25mm shells from the Bradleys could be heard impacting the upper stories. A calm descended on the first floor as the attackers realized there were no more defenders to use for targets. It had all the hold-your-breath anticipation of the eerie calm found in the eye of a hurricane.

When the stairwell doors opened Lisa and a dozen other leaders among the citizen soldiers hurriedly shouted "Hold your fire!!" as half naked and naked women stumbled out into the carnage of the first floor. The women were all in shock and almost incoherent, but by the time they had been escorted out of the building fragments of their tortured stories were feverishly making the rounds. Charging like a bull at a red cape, enraged Americans crashed their way into the many stairwells on the first floor and directly into the waiting massed fire of the Jihadis.

The first wave of Americans was cut down almost immediately falling like dominoes one after another. Their places were instantly taken by others and slowly step-by step they forced the Warriors up the stairs until they had made it to the second floor. Before they left the stairwell to run into a buzz saw of pre-prepared ambushes the Americans cleared the way with grenades.

Lisa was one of the first out of the stairwell. She ran through the door, immediately moved to her left, and hit the floor rolling behind a metal desk. She could hear the sounds of small arms fire hitting the other side of the desk, and she could see Americans falling as they ran out of the stairwell. The fallen were quickly replaced by others many of whom made it to cover and some who just stood there firing and somehow not getting hit. Looking under the desk she could see the feet and ankles of Warriors several desk rows beyond her. She maneuvered her AR-15 and sprayed the exposed limbs with fire. Three Warriors fell to the floor and Lisa squeezed off another burst this time hitting them in their face, neck, or other vital areas.

Thinking the way in that direction had been cleared Lisa jumped up and started leaping over desks. After the second desk, when she landed her ankle was grabbed by a Warrior who was hiding behind a big file cabinet. Lisa came down hard on her side. The Warrior grabbed her around the neck from behind and tried to pin her arms under her. As he rolled his entire weight on top of her he said, "Now you die you Unbeliever whore," in perfect English. Lisa was struggling to reach her knife when suddenly the man's hands went limp and he transitioned from a purposeful living human to the deadweight of a corpse.

Rolling the dead Warrior off her she could see the back half of his head was now a bleeding oozing wound. Looking up she saw a young girl, she couldn't have been more than fifteen, holding the 357 Magnum that had saved her life. She reached up and pulled the girl down beside her. "Thanks," she said knowing that would never be enough.

"They killed my Mom and Dad," the girl said in a flat voice that lacked any shade of emotion. The building rocked as several 25 mm rounds crashed through windows and exploded with devastating effect knocking down both Americans and terrorists.

"They killed my Mom and Dad," the girl said again. Then as Lisa tried to use her radio to order the Bradleys to start on the third floor the girl jumped up and started firing as she screamed "They killed my Mom and Dad!" Before Lisa could pull her down again a bullet found its mark and the girl crumpled to the floor like a rag doll with a bleeding hole where her face used to be.

The battle ebbed and flowed from cubicle to cubicle from desk to desk and office to office as a steady stream of Americans pushed their way onto the second floor in the face of steady but decreasing fire from the invaders. The constantly growing firepower of the American citizen soldiers eventually brought all resistance on the second floor to an end.

The stairwell from the second to the third floor became a kill box as the terrorists rolled hand grenades into the teeth of the first few waves that tried to force their way up. Climbing over dead and mangled bodies, stepping over lumps of bleeding flesh, that moments before formed parts of living breathing men and women, the Americans in their blind rage and eagerness to close with these murders pushed their way onto the third floor.

It mirrored the battle scene on the second floor except that on the third floor they came upon many rooms where patients had been confined and executed. Although after hearing the stories from the violated women it would have been hard to imagine anything making the level of anger any higher, this latest evidence of atrocities made the Americans even more ruthless and bold.

Sargent Bushings and the squad of men and women with him, after exiting a room filled with a dozen bodies of executed patients, cornered a group of terrorists in a break room. After a few minutes with no return fire it became evident the Jihadis were out of ammo. As the Americans walked towards them, two slit their own throats. One jumped up and rushed the Americans yelling, "Allah Akbar!" Bushings and a few others practically cut him in half with fire from their AK-15s. Then two others stood up with their hands in the air. One of them said in perfect English with a southern accent, "We surrender."

Sargent Bushings of the Washington DC PD who had spent a long and proud career protecting and serving others stepped up to the one who had spoken, pulled his pistol, and shot him in his left temple saying, "Go meet your virgins you murdering bastard!"

Blood, bones, and goo splashed all over his companion who hurriedly tried to pull his knife yelling, "Alla…." before shots from several of the Americans cut him down in a hail of gunfire.

In another part of the third floor Brian

Billingham was in hand-to-hand combat with a Jihadi in a room where they faced each other alone. They had both run out of ammo. With knives in hand they prepared to engage knowing that only one of them would leave alive.

The terrorist yelled "Allah Akbar" as he leapt towards Brian who yelled, "Die you son-of-a-bitch" in return. Then they were rolling around on the floor each trying to get the advantage. At first they seemed evenly matched. Both were big men, over six feet, both weighed over 240 pounds and both were battle hardened and well trained.

Smashing him against the floor the terrorist caused Brian to drop his knife which went flying. They rolled a few more times and the terrorist ended up on top. He was trying to stab Brian in the face pressing his knife with all his weight. While Brian with both his hands holding the knife at bay pushed up with as much strength as he had. The terrorist shifted his body forward to use more of his weight to press the knife home. This gave Brian just the opportunity he had been hoping for. He pushed his whole body up as hard as he could. As Brian rocked back under the weight of his assailant he used the extra couple of inches of space at his hips to wrap his legs around the head of the terrorist.

Smashing his knees into the man's ears and crossing his ankles he used this new leverage to pull the Jihadi backwards. Freeing one of his hands while still pushing as much as he could against the other man holding the knife, Brian jammed his thumb into the terrorist's eye as hard as he could. Instantly the terrorist let go of the knife and grabbed at the hand that was crushing his eye. The released knife fell almost straight down slicing a long jagged gash in Brian's cheek. Ignoring the pain from the cut Brian kept pushing into the man's eye until he felt it pop. Screaming in pain the man rolled off and away from Brian. Reaching around without looking Brian's freed hands searched for the fallen knife. When he found it he rolled towards the man and plunged the knife into his throat. Brian stood up. Ahmed Mochtata, a native of Syria who had once been a university professor and the peace-loving father of five sons who were all dead now from an American Bomb, lay gurgling in his own blood.

In another part of the third floor Lisa, with blood running freely down her left cheek from a piece of flying glass that hit her, was leading about a dozen men and women in an assault on the main enemy resistance around a secretarial pool in the middle of a large office in the center of the third floor. After a few moments the Americans began to notice there was no more firing coming from the center of the room. "Hold your fire," Lisa shouted above the din of the American fire.

Though they could hear almost constant firing from all around them as well as the crash of 25mm shells hitting the fourth floor once the people with Lisa stopped firing silence fell in the big office

Into the sudden semi-silence someone yelled, "We are out of ammo. We want to surrender."

"Stand up with your hands up and no weapons," Lisa called back.

Almost immediately five men stood up with their hands raised and no weapons. Lisa said, "Come out into the open area on this side of the desks and lay face down on the floor with your hands behind your heads."

The men filed out of the secretarial pool and lay down with their hands behind their heads.

Lisa and several others stood up and started walking around the desks they had been hiding behind when suddenly two other men jumped up inside the secretarial pool with AR-15s and started spraying the room with fire. Immediately two Americans were hit and dropped like mannequins knocked off a pedestal. A bullet caught Lisa in her left arm. It spun her around and she fell to the floor. The Jihadis on the floor had rolled towards desks seeking cover as they tried to pull pistols they had concealed in their belts.

One American threw a grenade into the secretarial pool. Several others, taking no thought to their own safety, stepped around the desks that gave them cover and methodically shot all five men as they rolled on the floor unable to get their guns out in time to return fire. Then the grenade went off, but not before the two Jihadis in the pool with the AR-15s were able to cut down every one of the Americans who had stepped out of cover in a rain of lead.

In scene after scene that repeated this mayhem and ferocity the third floor was finally secured and once again the Americans were fighting their way up the stairwell, this time to the fourth floor.

CHAPTER TWENTY-NINE

The Battle of Walter Reed:

Down the Rabbit Hole

The 13th Armored Brigade of the West Virginia National Guard easily rolled over the remnants of the ISIS terrorists that had once formed a formidable perimeter around Walter Reed Hospital.

The Warriors inside the building were dazed. The Hellfire missiles had shattered the building and there were fires in many places. In other places corridors were choked with debris or opening into nothing forty feet from the ground. The enemy Command Center in a large conference room on the third floor had taken a direct hit and was half buried. The dead and dying lay everywhere, blood and gore covered what was left of the walls, and the moans and cries of the wounded filled the air.

Abdal El Shallub the first Governor of the ISIS Province of America, handpicked and personally appointed by the Caliph himself, Abu Bakr al-Baghdadi was dead, crushed by a falling beam. General Malouf the Commander of the Second, Third, and Fourth Wave attacks was dead his body ripped into several chunks by the explosion. Bassam Kassab the Commander of Strike Force One, former bus driver in Kansas City who had lived in America for thirteen years as a sleeper for the Muslim brotherhood until he pledged allegiance to ISIS online last year, was with dead his skull smashed by a flying brick.

Surveying this scene of destruction and immediately grasping the new situation caused by the death of all these leaders Adan Kaib the second-in-command of Strike Force One stepped up and took control of the situation.

Seeing the row of communication stations were largely untouched by the explosion and the subsequent collapse of part of the roof, Adan moved forward with the details he had long known of the final act of this American passion play. "Halim command the guards to kill all the patients and tell those guarding the

Unbeliever whores to send about fifty who
have had their treatments out to the Crusaders
so they will know what we think of them and
their polluted country."

"Yes sir," said Halim as he began transmitting
the orders.

In Colonel Johnson's Humvee, which was
rolling onto the hospital property behind the
wall of armor that was the 13th Brigade,
Sargent Hubbs who was in the backseat
monitoring the enemy communications in the
building and spoke fluent Arabic said, "Colonel
the leader of the terrorists has just ordered the
execution of all the patients and said
something about sending a bunch of whores in
our direction."

Though he didn't know what "whores" was
code for Colonel Johnson knew what executing
patients was all about. They were all either
wounded active duty soldiers or vets. He was
not about to stand by while these heroes died
at the hands of enemies who never should
have been allowed in this country to begin
with. "Sargent Hubbs, radio Colonel Larson to
take the infantry into the building and clear out
the enemy with extreme prejudice."

"Yes sir," Sargent Hubbs replied turning quickly

to carry out his orders.

Moments later, after he had transmitted the orders to Lieutenant Colonel Larson and as the Infantry was running past their Humvee towards the smashed and smoking building, Hubbs said, "Sir I have Colonel Hodges of the 24th Armored on the line."

"Give me that headset. Billy Ray it's about time you got here. General Corbaine told me you would be coming. Is Hank Osborn and the 11th with you?" Colonel Johnson asked.

"No Hank was ordered to divert to Rockville to take back the town. From what I'm hearing it has turned into a real handful of crap. So it's just the fighting 13th and the mighty 24th just like it was that day in Al Hadihah in the Sand Box when all those Jihadis tried to take out your command post," answered Colonel Hodges.

"Only this time the Bedouins are on American soil. We just overheard them ordering the execution of all the patients and something about sending whores our way. I don't know what the hell they mean by whores but I dam well know what they mean about executing our wounded. I've sent in my infantry to clear these bastards out. Hopefully we'll be able to rescue some of our people" Colonel Johnson said as he watched his leading units fighting their way into the building.

"What do you want us to do Dave?" Colonel Hodges asked.

"Billy Ray, form a ring around the battle site. Don't let any of these terrorists get out when the fire gets too hot. Send half of your infantry in to support my guys."

"Will do Dave and Dave keep your head down,"

"And your guard up," Colonel Johnson finished the line they used to say to each other during battles back in Iraq.

Handing the headset back to Sargent Hubbs Dave itched to get into the fight but he knew he needed to stand back to provide command and control.

"Sir, Lieutenant Sorenson is reporting that a large number of American women are coming out of a stairwell on the first floor," reported Hubbs.

"Good maybe they've changed their minds or some cooler heads have prevailed and they're going to release the hostages" replied Colonel Johnson.

"I don't think that's it sir. Lieutenant Sorenson is reporting that the released prisoners are all women, they're mostly naked, and in bad shape" said Hubbs. "Now Lieutenant Sorenson reports he's sending the women to the rear and pressing the fight to clear the first floor.

Waiting until the women were clear both the terrorists and the Americans observed a brief cease fire which was shattered by a resumption of fire by the terrorists. Several Americans who had carelessly left cover and dropped their guard while they were dealing with the wounded and shell-shocked women were killed or wounded in the first burst of gunfire from the enemy.

Lieutenant George Sorenson who was an officer on the Charles Town West Virginia police force when he wasn't active with the Guard had an abiding hatred for Islamist terrorists. During his last tour in Iraq his two best friends Billy Anderson and James "Bubba" Siekes were both killed. Bubba had been captured. They found his bleeding and partially dismembered body hanging from a lamp post.

Seeing the battered and bruised bodies and the shame of humiliation in the tears of the women made his hatred rise to a blinding rage.

Firing as he ran he led his troops in a mad assault on the terrorist positions on the first floor. Jumping over fallen bodies and chairs Sorenson ran directly into the guns of the enemy and miraculously wasn't hit.

Men were falling all around him as he leapt over an improvised defensive wall of desks and tackled two Jihadis at once. His AK-15 was empty so he used it as a club. After he smacked one on the side of the head with the composite butt he shoved the barrel into the other man's left eye.

As his men poured over and around the wall of desks Sorenson went through the crowded bunch of defenders like a buzz saw. First with his pistol he shot men in the head, the chest, and anywhere he could until his gun was empty. Then he pulled his knife and began slicing and stabbing until there was no one left to kill.

Picking up an AK-15 from the floor and a few magazines from a dead soldier he called behind him, "Come on men let's get these bastards," as he started to his left where the last group of terrorists on the first floor were holding out.   Coming in behind, Sorenson's squad was able to cut them down and in short order the first floor was once again American territory.

Looking around and seeing that he was the senior man standing, Lieutenant Sorenson keyed the microphone that dangled from his left shoulder and said, "The first floor is secure. We're heading into the stairwells going up to the second floor.

Man after man fell at Sorenson's side as they battled their way up the stairwells and onto the second floor and still the man's luck held out. The second floor turned into a contest of who could best throw and who could who could best avoid hand grenades.   After many deaths and many wounds that would change lives forever the Americans won the contest. The second floor was secure.

The stairwells going up to the third and final floor had all been severely damaged by the hellfire missiles. The troopers of the 13th Brigade had to keep up a constant fire and in places they had to use ropes and their best climbing skills to make it to the next landing in the face of a determined and entrenched enemy. Luckily these were all West Virginia boys. They had grown up climbing mountains and running up slippery rocky paths.

It was a slow slog. It started to seem as if no

one could fight their way past the second landing in any of the stairwells.

"Colonel Johnson, Lieutenant Sorenson reports the men are stalled in the shattered stairwells leading from the second to the third floors and they may have to withdraw from the stairwells all together. He reports the terrorists are dropping hand grenades. The losses are becoming unsustainable" said Sargent Hubbs.

Tell him to pull back out of the stairwells and wait for reinforcements from the 24th to arrive."

"Yes sir," Hubbs responded before he transmitted the order to pull back.

Lieutenant Sorenson hated to pull back. Every fiber in his being wanted to get at these invaders who had desecrated this institution dedicated to healing America's wounded warriors. He knew they couldn't get up the shattered stairwells. He needed more men and another strategy.

Down on the ground in his command vehicle Colonel Johnson sent more men as he came up with another strategy. "Hubbs get Colonel Greenstein of the 337th Combat Aviation Brigade on the horn."

In a moment Hubbs was handing the headset to Johnson. "Colonel Greenstein my men are blocked by shattered stairwells between the second and third floors. Send your chinooks over to the 24th Armored in the second ring. Put as many infantry on them as you can and drop them on the roof."

"Yes, sir we'll make that end run for you," Greenstein answered.

Handing the headset back to Hubbs Colonel Johnson said, "Now get Colonel Hodges for me."

"Yes sir." Hubbs handed the headset to Colonel Johnson as soon as Hodges was on the line.

"Billy Ray I'm sending some chinooks to your location. Our men are held up by shattered stairwells. They can't get from the second to the third floor. Fill those chinooks. They'll drop your men on the roof. Take the third floor and let's wind this thing up."

"You've got it Dave! My men have been chomping at the bit to get in there and kill some of these no good terrorist scum."

Soon the chinooks were loading the men for the final assault not knowing they would go up on the roof only to go down the rabbit hole.

CHAPTER THIRTY

Tippecanoe and Parker Too

President Laura Parker and General Brown poured over maps of the Middle East planning for a great offensive to be launched from Jordan. Pointing at a map of Jordan she said, "General order every available troop we have in the entire region, and I mean Marines from the Fifth and Sixth fleets, all the advisors in Iraq, all the Special Ops, all hands on deck to rendezvous ASAP at the Jordanian Air Force base in Irbid. Communicate to all our allies, to Russia, to all the actors in the field that we're launching a full-scale invasion of Syria the moment we have the forces assembled. We're going to defeat these savages once and for all and finally bring peace to the world."

"Yes, Ma'am," said the General. He was on his

phone transmitting the appropriate orders when Mike Bender came into the room. He had just left a few moments before to convey the President's orders concerning the interrogation of prisoners.

"What is it Mike? Are some of those weak kneed bureaucrats giving you a hard time about getting rough with these murdering animals?"

"No, Madam President there's something else I need to talk to you about."

Turning back to study the maps the President asked, "What is it?"

"You might want to hear this in private," Mike replied.

Laura reflected on the fact that General Brown had told her he was in for the long haul and that he was even now conveying orders that could change the history of the world without once questioning her authority. Feeling she had no time to waste on political niceties or considerations she felt completely comfortable hearing whatever Mike had to say in front of General Brown so she said, "What is it Mike? You can speak freely in front of the General.

General Brown, who had spent years as the Commander of the U.S. Army Intelligence

Center was listening to what was transpiring even as he gave the orders for the invasion of a sovereign country and the intrusion of the United States into one of the deadliest civil wars in modern History.

With a quick look at the General and just a few seconds hesitation Bender said, "Madam President the Wisconsin National Guard refused to arrest Governor Runner and the Wisconsin State Police refused to shut down the radio station in Janesville. Governor Runner is on the air right now broadcasting from Madison and all the networks are carrying his speech. He's telling the whole country that you've arrested Speaker Bryan, that he's the rightful president, and that you've staged a coup and are illegally acting as the president."

By the time he finished speaking General Brown had conveyed the orders that set in motion a massive invasion of Syria.

Shaken by what she just heard Patricia Parker perhaps soon to be traitor and ex-president said, "That'll be all for now Mike. Give me a minute to speak with the General."

After Mike left the room these two main actors in America's coordinated response to this unbelievable day of invasion, murder, and mayhem stood silently looking at each other.

General Brown ever a political animal was calculating how he could, if not save his career, at least avoid jail.

Patricia Parker was a patriotic soul who had only entered politics to see if she could do something to stop America's slide into socialism and totalitarianism. After three years in office she was so disgusted with the corruption and egos of it all she had already announced that she would not seek re-election as the Governor of Arizona. Then came the surprise nomination from President Obonyo.

She knew the Progressive President only wanted to use her as a campaign prop. However, she had hoped that maybe with the added prestige she would gain by being a former cabinet member it would open doors for her to have a louder voice in the future. Then this day dawned. When she was informed by her staff that she was the next in line to be president, she didn't hesitate or equivocate and stepped-up. She took command and did what she thought was necessary to save the nation.

When she was told that the Speaker of the House was still alive she knew with the death of the President and Vice-President he was the legal heir to the office. That was when she made the fateful decision to ignore the law and retain the reins of power. She immediately came up with an argument saying that once she was legally sworn in she was legally the President. She knew she was on shaky ground arresting the Speaker. As she reflected on the situation in Wisconsin and that she may well be branded a traitor she made another decision. The country could not stand a break in command now. She was going to soldier on and come what may she would maintain her claim that she had been legally sworn in and was thus the legal President of the United States.

All of this flashed through her mind as a revelation. Before she could speak General Brown said, "Madam President perhaps we should release the Speaker and bring him into our counsels. We should at least acknowledge that we're aware of his rightful place in the chain of command and let the Supreme Court or Congress sort this all out after the battle is won."

Before she could answer a runner from the Communication Center knocked and entered, "Madam President General Zchevinsky reports that the jets have scrambled and they should be within firing range in about ten minutes. Also a General Vasquez with the 38th Light Infantry of the New Mexico National Guard has crossed the state border and is closing with the ISIS-Cartel column. He said he should make contact with the enemy in about half an hour."

"That's great news! Convey my thanks to Generals Zchevinsky and Vaquez" said the President.

"Yes Ma'am," said the runner as he turned to carry out the President's order.

Before he could get out of the door another runner from the Communications Center burst into the room and breathlessly announced, "Madam President the forward observers have told us the ISIS-Cartel column has entered firing range and they're deploying their self-propelled and towed howitzers.

"Madam President the 105 MM and 106 MM Howitzers the Mexicans have can fire as many as four rounds per minute, so even without GPS guidance they'll be able to destroy the hundred acres of this base. We need to take shelter immediately."

As he finished speaking the sound of artillery impacts could be heard from several directions.

"Lead the way General," the President said. She started to follow General Brown who had been on the base for years and knew where the shelters were when the building shook with the first impact.

The President was running behind the General towards the closest shelter with ceiling tiles falling and dust filling the rooms as more and more thunderous impacts could be heard landing in all directions. They were only yards from the door to the shelter; a young Lieutenant was holding the massive steel door open saying, "Hurry Madam President, Hur…" when the opening to the shelter took a direct hit. The flying metal shards from the door and blasted pieces of bricks from the wall nearly shredded the bodies of President Patricia Parker, General Edward Brown, and everyone else in the area. Then the roof collapsed and the curtain came down on the shortest presidential administration in American History.

CHAPTER THIRTY-ONE

Humpty Dumpty Sat On a Wall

In the dust and debris filled interior of Walter Reed Hospital the men and women of the West Virginia National Guard still had visions of the battered and abused women the Jihadis had released after the first floor was cleared. The echoes of their pitiful stories enraged the passions of the troops as they battled their way to and through the second floor.

The battle to get up the stairwells from the second to the third floor saw acts of heroism and gallantry as great as any seen in other American wars. Countless soldiers, who if the truth was ever known, should have received the Congressional Medal of Honor for actions above and beyond the call of duty fought on selflessly many finding only death or lifelong disability as the reward.

National Guard units made up as they are of people from a certain location aren't like regular army formations. Everyone knows each other, often for their whole lives. Their kids go to school together. They attend the same churches and work in the same factories and businesses. They are more than a band of brothers. They are friends. So there were many instances were lifelong friends and neighbors watched as those closest to them were killed and wounded. There is a rising tide of warlike energy that possesses the souls of all involved in pitched battles. In this great Battle of Walter Reed it swirled like a snownado in a whiteout: a force invisible and invincible that motivated these weekend warriors to do things no one else would have even attempted.

Lieutenant Colonel Bobby Larson led several squads into one of the shattered stairwells leading from the second to the third floor. He had been ordered to keep the enemy busy as a diversion for the air assault on the third floor. He entered the stairwell and was firing up at the next landing when he thought his life was over. He saw a grenade land at his feet. He instinctively covered his face and jumped back to fall over a pile of bodies made up of people he had known since grade school. Just before the grenade exploded Tommy Van Schoorel jumped on it and absorbed the blast. Bobby lay there alive and unhurt thinking, "And we used to make fun of Tommy for being such a sissy. My God what a hero."

Corporal Johnny Stewart a boyhood friend and the brother of Larson's wife reached down and gave Bobby a hand up, "Come on Bobby, you can't take a lay down now," he said with a smile.

Bobby lived right down the street from the Colonel and unless they were in a formal situation like many people in the Brigade they didn't stand on ceremony. Thinking of the many scrapes and fights they had been in together growing up on the wrong side of the tracks in Charles Town Bobby said "Thanks Johnny you've always been pulling me out of .." The bullet entered the back of Johnny's neck in the small space between his helmet and his flak jacket that was exposed because of the awkward position he was in straddling a body and leaning forward to help Bobby up.

Bobby screamed, "No!" in horror as his best friend and brother-in-law's face exploded showering him with gore that had once been the boy next door. Bobby still didn't have his feet under him and he fell backwards with the dead weight of Johnny's body on top of him. In his pain and loss Bobby hugged Johnny saying, "No...No..No"

In another stairwell on the other side of the building Lieutenant George Sorenson now armed with a M249 light machine gun or SAW led several squads of men out onto what was left of a platform. He was holding the SAW with both hands. The long belt of ammunition trailed to the floor and rattled its way up to the firing chamber as he laid down a continuous fire to suppress the terrorists from seeing where to throw their grenades or aim their rifles. Two men who tried to help by feeding the belt or handing him another had already died from ricochet hits.

Bodies of both guardsmen and Jihadis lay in heaps around Sorenson's feet as he yelled, "Come on you Bastards get yourself some of this!" He fired until the barrel of the M249 was starting to glow red and he knew it was about to begin jamming. He threw down the light machine gun and pulled his pistol. He emptied all fifteen rounds from the first magazine in his 40 caliber Glock 22. He dropped the magazine and slammed another in place. He could hear

the roar and the deep
"Thump...Thump...Thump" that could only be
Chinooks landing on the roof.

Thinking of Billy and Bubba and how they died
Lieutenant George Sorenson emptied his
second magazine. After slamming a third into
place he was once again firing up the stairwell
yelling, "This one's for Bubba." "This one's for
Billy" over and over as he fired. Then a mighty
roar punctured both his ear drums quickly
followed by fire and smoke streaming down the
stairwell. The entire building collapsed on top
of him and all the men of the 13th Armored
Brigade.

Thousands including Lieutenant Colonel Bobby
Larson and Lieutenant George Sorenson died
immediately crushed under the collapsing
floors of Walter Reed Hospital. Hundreds more
who were closely surrounding the building
were also killed in the initial explosion. Many
more would die later from their wounds and
more than another thousand would carry the
wounds into lives forever altered by their
injuries. Many others would later be diagnosed
with a form of Ground Zero respiratory
illnesses and cancer from breathing the
noxious fumes released in the collapse of the
building.

The wound on Lisa's left arm was starting to saturate and bleed through the handkerchief she had someone tie around her left arm. From her paramedic training she knew she was losing enough blood that it was eventually going to knock her out and then kill her if she didn't get it stopped. There just wasn't time.

Looking about the shattered remains of what had once been a world-class hospital she thought, "The third floor is clear but we still have to get to the fourth floor to clean out this nest of snakes." Looking at the dead and the wounded she could see that this fight had already taken a frightful toll on these citizen soldiers who spontaneously rose up to assault battle hardened and trained Warriors in the protection of their homes and their Homeland.

She was wondering, "Do we have enough people still able to fight? We may have to just hold on until more help arrives." Just then help arrived. It arrived in the form of soldiers from the 66th Infantry of the Maryland National Guard. From where she sat slumped on a desk she could see the soldiers coming out of the stairwell from the second floor.

She was just about to get up and go over to

ask who they were when she noticed that an officer was talking to Sargent Bushings who was sitting in a big leather chair by one of the stairwell doors. In a moment she could see the Sargent point at her and the officer followed by a sergeant and a few other soldiers headed her way.

"I was told that you're Colonel Edwards," said a captain who looked to be about the same age as Lisa.

Not used to or very comfortable with being addressed as Colonel Lisa answered, "Well Captain that's who they tell me I am."

"I'm Captain Roberts of the 66th Infantry of the Maryland National Guard and I've been ordered to coordinate with you in this assault."

"Captain as you can see these civilians are about spent, and we still need to fight our way up the stairwells to the fourth floor to get at the leaders of these ISIS invaders. So if you and your men can help us get at them let's go cut off the head of this snake," Lisa said.

Looking at the blood running down Lisa's left arm and at the way she was leaning over and holding it he said, "Colonel you look like you might want to consider staying here or better yet going down to an aid station."

"I've no intention of leaving this fight until we finish the job," Lisa said. "How many men do you have Captain?"

"We have 5000 in our Brigade and our commander Colonel Givens has sent two battalions with close to a thousand soldiers into the building to assist you," answered Captain Roberts.

Standing up Lisa kept one hand on the desk to steady herself. "All right Captain let's form up and get up to the fourth floor and end this thing." Calling out to the big room filled with the exhausted and in many cases wounded citizen soldiers who had fought this far with her Lisa yelled, "Heads up everybody, heads up!" In the din of conversation and the sound of firing that was still going on outside into the fourth floor her voice, never loud and now cracking from strain and smoke, was largely ignored.

She was startled when behind her and out of her line of sight Captain Roberts raised a whistle to his lips and blew it very loudly. This was greeted with silence into which she spoke, "I want those who've fought this far to remain here and hold the third floor. You've done what I'm sure just yesterday none of us thought we could do. We've taken back three quarters of this vast hospital from terrorists. But now you're exhausted and we need to use these fresh troops from the National Guard who're here to help."

Turning to the Captain Lisa said, "There's the plan Captain. I want these heroes to stay here and rest on their laurels while you and your men follow me up to the fourth floor."

"Are you sure you don't want to follow your own advice. If you won't go down and get that wound treated stay here and let us finish this job," Captain Roberts said.

She might not have been used to being a colonel. And she may never have risen above the rank of E-8. But she knew that she had been promoted to colonel and that a colonel outranked a captain so she had an authoritative ring in her voice when she said, "This isn't a debate Captain. I'm going to lead this assault."

"Yes Ma'am," the Captain replied, "How shall we proceed?"

"Just follow me and don't stop shooting until all these ISIS assholes are dead."

Steadying herself by an act of will Lisa walked to the nearest door leading to the stairwell up to the fourth floor. When she got to the door she waited until the knot of men following her and Captain Roberts grew into a throng and then into a mass of men eager to take the fight to the enemy. Looking around she saw that the same thing was developing at each stairwell door. When she thought it looked like enough for a credible assault she yelled, "Charge!" and led the way into the stairwell.

On the fourth floor in the Command Center Abduhl Baroun the Commander of Strike Force Three stood stone faced as Hisham Mikhail his second-in-command reported, "Sir the Crusaders have begun their push up the stairwells from the third floor."

"Dump all the grenades we have left upon their heads. Kill all of the Unbeliever dogs you can. When they reach the second landing let judgment come upon them."

As Hisham walked away to carry out his orders Abduhl remembered the day he had been recruited for this glorious mission. It was last summer right after his whole village had been leveled by the air force of that hated puppet of the crusaders the Zindiq dog Bashar al-Assad. His wife and eight children had been killed as they ran for cover from a barrel bomb.

The resolve to kill as many of the American Crusaders as he could grew to a raging fire as he thought, "I was off fighting for the Caliph against the Shia dogs in Iraq. I came home not to my loving family but to graves already grown cold."

The sounds of gun fire and hand grenades echoed up the stairwells mixed with the shouts of Warriors and the cries of the wounded. The smell of burning electrical wiring mixed with the dust of a building wracked and ruined by battle formed a toxic cloud that would have long lasting effects on all who breathed it and survived. Now a constant fire was smashing windows as ground fire from the many soldiers surrounding the building did their best to keep the defenders of the fourth floor pinned down. They didn't know that most of the Warriors, the communication techs, and the members of the leadership were already dead or dying. Only a few active Warriors kept the Americans from breaking through. The nature of fighting up a stairwell being what it was it only takes a few to hold back many.

Lisa, followed by Captain Roberts was still in the fight leading their soldiers up one step at a time. Lisa had been wounded a second time. This time it was a jagged cut on her right cheek where a piece of flying masonry had cut her face knocking her to the ground. Captain Roberts helped her up and they continued fighting.

The dropping grenades were killing and wounding whole squads at a time, but more and more soldiers kept pushing their way in over dead bodies and piles of wounded. Finally just as they reached the second landing they heard shouts of "Allah Akbar! Allah Akbar!" and then as far as they were concerned the world ended.

A tremendous explosion caused by the simultaneous detonation of hundreds of pounds of plastic explosives shook the building. This was all wired together and placed in every room and hallway of the fourth floor as well as down the stairwells between the second and the third landing. The men and women who were fighting in the stairwells never knew what hit them. Those on the first, second, and third floors had a moment of wonder and then of panic as the building crashed in upon itself killing nearly every person within. Some escaped with life changing injuries but most died in the crush.

Outside hundreds more died in the immediate explosion and thousands later succumbed to wounds and other complications as the once proud St. Elizabeth Hospital, a landmark in Washington, DC since its founding in 1855, came crashing down.

Mitch and the Patriots were making headway. The Warriors fought for every office, hallway, cubicle, and desk as inch-by-inch foot-by-foot and yard-by-yard the Americans killed, wounded or incapacitated the terrorists. Few survived falling into the hands of the enraged citizens of a free republic under attack by the Islamists. Most were shot where they fell. Some were rounded up and sent down as prisoners though few of these made it all the way out before they were summarily shot. In this battle of cultures there was no quarter given and none asked. After the Patriots saw or heard what had been done to the women captives almost every one of them had no qualms about shooting wounded or unarmed ISIS Warriors.

It was on the fourth floor where Junior Williams found himself in a hand-to-hand struggle with a terrorist. They met in a small office. After throwing a few rounds at each other from behind desks they both ran out of ammunition. Rolling around locked in a life and death struggle the terrorist proved himself to be both stronger and a better man with a knife.   First he managed to give Junior a slicing wound on his right thigh. Then recovering from a punch Junior landed on his left ear, the terrorist was able to slide his blade between the front and back pads of Junior's flak vest. The razor sharp blade hit a rib and then sliding between two others found Junior's heart and he died instantly as the Warrior shoved hard and then twisted his blade.

He was kneeling next to Junior's body wiping the blade on Junior's pant leg and searching his body for ammo when Billy Hill and a few others from Dinwiddie stepped into the room. The man tried to get off his knees but he never made it as all of their guns tore him apart. Billy Hill ran to his friend's body and closing Junior's eyes he swore that he would never rest until every ISIS savage in the world was dead.

On the sixth floor Mitch found himself in the same room as his wife Joan and his son Billy. They all entered the big central room from different directions. After a ferocious fire fight cleared the space of terrorists they had a brief reunion in the center of the room.

Mitch and Joan hugged holding on to each

other. "I love you," said Joan with tears in her eyes.

"I love you more," responded Mitch.

Then both of them reached out an arm and pulled their son Billy into a group hug. "If only Junior was here we could call this a family reunion," Mitch said.

Having come into the room where Junior died right after Billy Hill and the other men from Dinwiddie Billy knew what had happened to Junior. At his father's words Billy teared up and said, "Junior didn't make it. Some Jihadi bastard killed him in a hand-to-hand fight."

"Oh my God," Joan sobbed as she dropped to her knees. "Oh my God what are we going to do," she said as tears flowed down her cheeks.

Dropping to his knees Mitch hugged his wife. He and Joan had only been twenty years old when Junior was born. They were stationed in Germany and the next few years were some of the happiest they had ever known. Junior had always been the golden boy not just of their nuclear family but of the extended family as well: the first grandchild, the first nephew, the captain of the football team, and the king of the senior prom. He had married his high school sweetheart. Everyone in Dinwiddie loved Junior. Though he was still young but he was already part of a long southern tradition. In the hearts and minds of all who knew him Junior had been a Good ol' Boy.

In the midst of the death and destruction of America's deadliest day since the Battle of the Argonne Forest in 1918 two people both intimately involved in a great and bloody battle forgot all about that and held each other as they grieved the loss of their son.

Through his own pain he knew that this was a moment of great loss for his parents so Billy said, "You two stay here, you've done enough. I'm returning to the fight.   We still have two more floors to clear."

Suddenly feeling old and drained of strength Mitch was about to agree with Billy when Joan said, "No way. I want to see the last one of these murdering ISIS bastards when he draws his last breath so I can shoot him one more time for Junior."

Mitch was shocked by the ferocity he heard in Joan's voice. He had known her all his life. He had loved her for most of it, and he knew her to be the sweetest most loving person he had ever known. She was a model mother who had carted the kids to and from football and soccer, baked the best berry pies in the county, and loved life with all her heart. He could well understand her thirst for revenge. He felt it himself. He was just surprised to hear his petite little soulmate sound so deadly.

Standing up the three moved back into the battle. Picking up extra magazines and hand grenades off fallen Warriors they were soon jumping over bodies and firing up. Always up as they and the other Patriots made their way up the stairwell from the sixth to the seventh floor. On the seventh floor as they were attacking a group of Jihadis that were pinned down behind a make-shift wall of tipped over desks Billy rose up a little too high to throw a hand grenade and just as he was about to let it fly he was hit in the shoulder.

Spinning around and falling, Billy dropped the grenade with no pin which was about to explode. Joan jumped over to Billy and cradled him in her lap, crying out, "No! No!" Mitch reached out and grabbed the grenade and flipped it towards the terrorists. It didn't make it all the way. When it exploded in the air over their heads the burning shrapnel knocked them out of the fight long enough for some other Patriots to run up from the other side of the room and with a long burst of fire from their AR 15s and take them out.

Billy wasn't so badly hurt that he was going to die but he was hurt bad enough to knock him out of the fight. The losses among the Virginia Patriots were high and constantly growing higher. Most of the Dinwiddie Patriots were either dead or out of action. However, their ranks were being expanded constantly as more and more soldiers from the 47th Infantry Virginia National Guard came in to help in the assault. The building was packed with enraged Americans just itching to get close enough to kill one of these invaders.

Just like so many other times in their wonderful, loving, fulfilling twenty-nine years of marriage Mitch and Joan Williams were side by side. Only this time they weren't sharing a family moment, working to make a better life for themselves and their children, nor were they looking lovingly into each other eyes as they repeated their favorite toast, "All because two people are still in love." No, this time they were side by side fighting their way up a crowded stairwell from the seventh to the eighth floor in the Virginia Hospital Center in Arlington, Virginia when like a bolt of lightning in a clap of thunder the stairwell and the entire eighth floor exploded so powerfully that it could be heard, seen, and felt miles away.

The building came down as if it was made of Legos that had a bowling ball dropped on it. Bricks and steel girders shattered, melted, and flew in all directions. The main portion of the building shuddered and then sagged in upon itself trapping the thousands of Patriots and soldiers who were inside in what became a death trap. Anyone within fifty yards of the building was dead. In concentric circles spreading out from the epicenter the injuries changed the lives of thousands. For the first time since 1865 war had come to the Old Dominion.

General Rick Stamper sat at his desk in the VH-3D Sea King Helicopter that he had commandeered from Andrews Air Force base. The machine had been specially fitted out for the use of the President and had served several times as Marine One. In this large helicopter Stamper had the best communications available as well as superior defensive and offensive capabilities.

"General Stamper we're receiving reports that both St. Elizabeth's and the Virginia Hospital Center have exploded as our guys were about to reach the top floor just like Walter Reed," said Sargent Julie Barns.

Sitting across his desk was Colonel Ben Summers the commander of the 101st Combat Aviation Brigade which Stamper had ordered in from Langley Air Force Base in Hampton Virginia. Reacting to the news of what was happening in the different battel sites Stamper said, "Ron if I pull all my men out of the Adventist Hospital can your boys bring the place down around the Jihadis heads?"

"Yes sir we sure can. Have your men fall back at least one hundred yards and take cover. My Apaches and our Hellfire missiles will give you one hell of a burning crater where that Hospital is standing right now," answered Captain Rogers.

"Sargent Barns get me Lieutenant Colonel Smith on the horn."

"Yes sir," said Sargent Barnes as she left to contact the joint Delta-SEAL team in the field.

In a moment Sargent Barnes returned to announce "The team leadership is on line one, sir."

Picking up the phone on his desk he hit the speaker button and said, "Huffy, what's the situation there?'

"Sir this is Captain Grady, Colonel Smith is dead and Captain Sarraf is badly wounded so I'm senior officer in command."

"All right Jim what's the situation."

"We've cleared six floors and we're fighting our way up the stairwell from the sixth to the seventh floor right now. It has been rough sir. These Jihadis are well trained and well equipped. They aren't giving up without a fight for each room and desk. Our men are doing their duty and then some. The police and civilians who've showed up to help have filled the ranks and fought like tigers, sir. And sir after we cleared the first floor the terrorists sent out about fifty women, most of them naked and badly beaten. They were all raped General. They said the Terrorists sent them out to tell us what they were going to do to all our women. And they shot all the patients sir."

Feeling a deep regret that his longtime friend Huffy Smith had bought the farm but shoving that sadness down for another day as well as a deep rage for the way these invaders were treating American women and helpless patients Stamper said, "Jim I want you to stop the assault immediately and pull back. Pull all your men out and move back at least one hundred yards then take cover."

"But we can take that top floor sir I know we can," responded Captain Grady.

"I have no doubt that you can Jim but here's what's happening. At the other three sites as soon as our guys reached about half way up the stairwells to the top floor the ISIS murders blew the buildings."

"We haven't seen any charges. There have been plenty of booby traps, but we've seen no evidence that the building has been wired," Grady said.

"They haven't set the whole building to blow just the top floor and the top half of all the stairwells. They're using enough c-4 to take down the whole building when the top blows up and collapses. So get your men out of there. Let me know when you make cover and we'll have the Apaches bring the damn place down around their ears," Stamper said.

"Yes sir we'll begin evacuating the building immediately."

"Good work today Grady, be safe and get my men out of there," ordered Stamper.

Yes sir," responded Grady as he moved immediately to follow his orders.

About ten minutes later American regular and citizen soldiers were streaming out of every door, window, and hole in the wall and running away from the building. Small rear guard units were keeping the Jihadis from coming back down the stairwells to attack the retreating Americans.

On the top floor Hussain El Komar second-in-command of Strike Force Two approached his commander Mahamoud Abzaak and said, "Brother the Crusaders have stopped their advance up the stairwells and their soldiers are fleeing the building in every direction."

"They must have learned of our plan to send them to Hell as we go to Paradise," replied Mahamoud.

Calling out as loudly as he could the Commander of Strike Force Two addressed the room. It was filled with men who had plotted and planned this attack. Men he had known through good and bad. They were his band of brothers. "My brothers, the Crusaders have learned of our ultimate surprise and the cowards are fleeing as I speak. I will now throw the switch and send them all to Hell. I will see you this day in Paradise."

Shouts of "Allah Akbar! Allah Akbar" filled the room. Their leader, Mahamoud Abzaak heard the shouts with a feeling of fulfillment. He was a former doctor whose career of helping the needy ended one day when an American plane dropped a five hundred pound bomb on his home compound. It killed his entire extended family at his oldest daughter's wedding by mistake. They were supposed to bomb his neighbor who was a Jihadi commander. After the funerals of his loved ones he moved in with his neighbor and started his journey to the Adventist Hospital in Washington, DC.

With the victorious shouts of his brothers in his ears Mahamoud threw the switch that set off almost a thousand pounds of C-4 placed strategically all over the eighth floor. The blast shattered windows half a mile away. The firestorm it created flashed down the stairwells and consumed the rear guard units before they knew what happened. About a third of the Americans had exited the building. Several hundred were far enough away that the blast and the concussion didn't kill them immediately. Hundreds who initially survived were doomed to die later after lingering for weeks and sometimes months. Others sustained life changing debilitating injuries. Still others would later be diagnosed with respiratory diseases and cancers that would be linked to the massive blast.

CHAPTER THIRTY-TWO

All the Kings Horses and All the Kings Men

Believing that continuity trumps constitutionality the advisors and bureaucrats who were creating the Bryan Administration on the fly counseled the new president not to repudiate the legality of what Patricia Parker had accomplished during the invasion of America.

Instead they counseled the new president that new circumstances required new reactions. They quickly moved to have their perennial supporters in the Corporations Once Known as the Mainstream Media burry any further mention of the incarceration of Peter Bryan by President Parker. They scrubbed the internet of any previous mention from a major source.

Then they counseled him to validate the one

day reign of Patricia Parker by confirming her appointments in the military realm and by getting behind the actions they had taken to assault ISIS worldwide so he could get in front of the parade and make sure the next wins go in the Bryan column.

The new president, former Speaker of the House Peter Bryan, was if anything a career politician. If he knew how to do anything he knew how to do what his consultants, advisors, and staff told him to do. He had spent his entire adult working life immersed in Washington politics. He had been a legislative aide, a staffer, and a speechwriter. He did have a one year-long hiatus from government employment as a marketing consultant in a family owned business so he could say he came from the private sector when he ran for Congress the first time. When he was first elected he became the youngest man to have ever served as a Representative in the House.

At his first national address as president Peter Bryan stood behind a podium with the seal of the President of the United States on it. He was in front of a backdrop the color of the blue in our flag with the word President over and over separated by white stars. There were walls of American flags on the edges of the

platform. Behind him stood General
Zchevinsky, Chief of Staff of the Air Force;
Admiral Davis, Chief of Naval Operations;
General Ogdan, Commandant of the Marine
Corps; General Wilson, *Chief* of the National
Guard Bureau; and General Rick Stamper, the
Supreme Commander at the Battle of
Washington.

As all America listened, the new president
looking directly into the camera as he read
from his teleprompter, "My Fellow Americans I
come before you tonight as your new
president. We all mourn the passing of
President Obonyo and so many others in our
government. I promise you I will honor my
oath to uphold and protect the Constitution
and I will work tirelessly to enrich and fulfill the
American dream of limited government,
personal liberty, and economic opportunity for
all people.

Never before has America been assaulted in
such a massive way. Never since the war of
1812 has an enemy touched the inner sanctum
of America: Washington, DC.

First the news: All the battles fought on
American soil yesterday were victories. Here
in Washington, in the four towns that were
briefly taken by the ISIS savages, along our

highways and byways, in countless other places across the continent, in each and every place due to the heroism of our Armed Forces and the willingness of our people to become citizen soldiers we have prevailed. In each and every place the enemy has been defeated, peace has been restored, and once again we stand united in the face of unprovoked aggression and determined to fight through to the ultimate victory, the final and everlasting defeat of worldwide terrorism.

Yesterday was the day beyond infamy. Yesterday America was assaulted by the cowardly assassins of a corrupt ideology. These savages who have hijacked a religion of peace and who have nothing to do with true Islam perpetrated the greatest crime in the History of the world.

They used our own generosity against us. Under the guise of refugees snuck in to become a dagger in our heart. And to prove to them that we are not afraid and we will not be changed by their cowardly attacks we will not only continue our refugee program we will double the number of refugees we accept from Syria.

Today tens of thousands mourn the loss of beloved family members, close friends, and neighbors. We all mourn the loss of President Obonyo, the Vice-President, and so many of our other martyred leaders. We mourn the loss of President Patricia Parker whose administration, though it may have been short, will live forever in the annals of American leadership and in the hearts and minds of all who owe her a tremendous debt of gratitude. She stepped up, restored the chain-of-command, and led us to victory. We all mourn the loss of tens of thousands of our innocent countrymen. And as we grieve a steely resolve has entered our bones.

A resolve to avenge this horrendous attack. To bring down all the might of the United States and its many allies upon the head of this vicious snake that tries to masquerade as a Caliphate.

A resolve to not allow this assault by barbarians within our gates to change us, to make us turn our backs on what America has always stood for.

A resolve to move forward with firm steps on our progressive journey to a better world.

With these resolves clearly in sight and deep within our hearts first of all I declare a thirty day period of national mourning. However in this call for national mourning while we will most assuredly reflect on all that has happened we must make sure that as an open and pluralistic society we do not allow the anti-American sentiments of Islamophobia to mar the honor of our fallen. I urge all Americans to remember that Islam is a religion of peace and these ISIL criminals have nothing to do with true Islam.

Second, I declare America's commitment to adhere to and enforce the protocols of the Paris Agreement on our way to a realistic plan to save our nation from the impending doom of global warming. The rising seas and choking air of our dying world are one of the prime causes of terrorism. There is no more courageous thing we can do than build a sustainable green world were all mankind can live in peace.

Third, in order to maintain order I am issuing an executive order declaring martial law. Later today every network and every broadcast and internet outlet in this country will transmit the new regulations and penalties designed to keep us safe. If you have any questions you will be able to report to your local police stations. They will explain everything you will need to know.

Fourth, to kick start the economy and to fight inflation after this tremendous shock I am issuing an executive order directing the Federal Reserve to immediately make two trillion dollars available for the rebuilding of our infrastructure.

Fifth, since this is obviously the greatest example that has ever occurred of domestic gun violence, and since we can no longer wait for Congress to pass common sense gun control that go beyond the actions taken by President Obonyo, I am issuing an executive order instituting common sense gun control for a modern era. The new regulations require all private gun owners to surrender their weapons to their local police officials. They will have thirty days to do so. Any civilian found in possession of a weapon after that date will be guilty of a felony. The penalties for the guilty as well as for anyone who participates in the concealment of any weapons will include confiscation of any property on which the weapons are found, confiscatory fines, and mandatory jail time of not more than twenty and not less than ten years.

Finally, turning to foreign affairs and our vigorous response to this unprovoked attack, our Armed Forces are at this moment entering

Mexico. They will destroy any ISIS training camps, capture or kill any cartel members, and obliterate their facilities. In the Mideast acting in conjunction with our many allies, including Russia and Iran, we are advancing into Syria from multiple fronts. The enemy capital of Raqqa has been carpet bombed into oblivion. Every terrorist training camp and every known terrorist formation has been hit by our air and naval forces. The remaining forces of the ISIL animals are concentrating near a town north of Damascus. There they will be encircled and destroyed. This battle is shaping up as I speak. I anticipate that by tomorrow I will be once again before you to announce our overwhelming victory at the Battle of Deraa.

May all of you rest easy tonight knowing that your government is taking action to save the planet, enforce common sense gun control, and punish our enemies. And may God bless the United States of America."

All the battles fought on American soil were declared to be victories. No American felt victorious. Our freedoms had been assaulted, our people had been killed, but we were told we should rest easy. At the end of the day to end all days, one empty suit replaced another empty suit. He has comforted us by invoking the Progressive incantation, "I'm from the government and I'm here to help."

May God bless the United States of America.

Disclaimer

This book is a work of fiction. Any similarity between characters in this book and any persons living or dead is in the mind of the reader and not the intention of the author. It is not meant to depict any expected events or to portray any actual plans, procedures or processes of the United States or its enemies. All of the military formations and their weapons components mentioned in this book are fictional and they are not intended to represent any actual United States Military formations either past or present.

Dr. Robert Owens is a College Professor and Administrator. He is the author of a widely published weekly opinion column which can be viewed at www.drobertowens.com. He is also a retired house painter, a retired pastor, a member of House Church Networks, an author and a composer. He holds an Associate Degree in Biblical Studies, a Bachelor Degree in Religious Education, a Bachelor Degree in History, a Master's Degree in Religious Education, a Master's Degree in History, and a Ph. D. in Organizational Leadership. Dr. Owens teaches History, Political Science, Religion, and Leadership. His books include; *Political Action Follows Political Philosophy*, *Colonial American History: The Essential Story*, *The Constitution Failed*, *The Azusa Street Revival*, *America Won the Vietnam War!* and *NEVER FORGET!* All these books are available online from Amazon.com, Barnes and Nobles.com and numerous other outlets.

Dr. Robert Owens